PRAISE FOR VIVIAN AREND

"If you've never read a Vivian Arend book you are missing out on one of the best contemporary authors writing today."
~ *Book Reading Gals*

"With sassy, spirited and familiar characters, Vivian Arend invites the readers to bear witness to the love and commitment of the characters we love."
~ *The Reading Cafe*

"Brilliant, raw, imaginative, irresistible!!"
~ *Avon Romance*

"The Heart Falls series is such a funny and sexy contemporary series, and I highly recommend to fans of contemporary romance."
~ *Blogging by Liza*

"Arend became a favorite author of mine because not only does she write about sexy cowboys, she gives us families who love and take care of each other."
~ *SmexyBooks*

"This was my first Vivian Arend story, and I know I want more!"
~ *Red Hot Plus Blue Reads*

ALSO BY VIVIAN AREND

Heart Falls Vignette & Novella Collection

Three Weddings and a Baby

Girls' Night Out

Rose's One Night to Forever

Fern's Date with Destiny

Hot Times in Heart Falls

The Stones of Heart Falls

A Rancher's Heart

A Rancher's Song

A Rancher's Bride

A Rancher's Love

A Rancher's Vow

The Colemans of Heart Falls

The Cowgirl's Forever Love

The Cowgirl's Secret Love

The Cowgirl's Chosen Love

A full list of Vivian's print titles is available on her website:
www.vivianarend.com

FERN'S DATE WITH DESTINY

A HEART FALLS NOVELLA

VIVIAN AREND

This is a work of fiction. Names, characters, places, and incidents either are the product of the author's imagination or are used fictitiously, and any resemblance to any persons, living or dead, business establishments, events, or locales is entirely coincidental.

NO AI TRAINING: Without in any way limiting the author's [and publisher's] exclusive rights under copyright, any use of this publication to "train" generative artificial intelligence (AI) technologies to generate text is expressly prohibited. The author reserves all rights to license uses of this work for generative AI training and development of machine learning language models.

Fern's Date with Destiny
Copyright © 2025 by Arend Publishing Inc.
Digital ISBN: 978-1-998508-53-2
Print ISBN: 978-1-998508-54-9
Edited by Angie Ramey
Cover Design © Damonza
Proofed by Linda Levy

INTERLUDE

The annual July 1ˢᵗ bachelor auction in Heart Falls had been the starting point for dozens of short-term relationships, a whole series of happily-ever-afters, and a few spectacular *oh my God* disasters.

This year promised to be one for the books as Cody Gabrielle stepped onto the stage, and the already wild crowd gathered in the community hall sucked in a collective, noisy breath.

Fern Fields didn't breathe.

She couldn't.

Because while he'd threatened to sign up, heck, she'd *told* him to, Cody wasn't supposed to be here. In the lineup. In the spotlight.

Not after what they'd shared. Not after she'd laid everything on the line.

He was dressed as if he hadn't intended to be onstage. His work jeans were clean but faded, and his old, soft black button-down was rolled to the elbows, displaying firm forearms. His deep brown hair was damp and stuck up in all directions as if he'd run a hand through it just before walking out.

Fern's dad was backstage behind the curtain, but right there on the stage, co-emcee Chance Gabrielle stumbled as he stared at his brother, a soft curse escaping at what was clearly not part of the original plan.

Cody and Chance exchanged a few words, too low for earshot. Around her, people whispered, nudging one another, trying to catch up. Seated beside her in the traditional metal and faux-leather community hall chairs, her sister Rose clutched her hand, but Fern felt nothing. Heard nothing, even though Chance was speaking now. Explaining, probably attempting to make the unreasonable reasonable.

Her heart pounded too loud, a bass drum of disbelief and something that might've been hope. Or fear.

Or fury. She hadn't decided yet.

Cody's eyes found hers as if by magic, and the rest of the room blurred into shadow. Time stretched as Fern stared back, hoping for a glimmer of understanding.

His left hand twitched, and he pressed it firmly to his thigh as if he didn't trust it to stay still.

Her heart ached. *Oh, Cody.*

He cleared his throat then lifted the mic his brother had passed to him.

"Hi," Cody said, voice low and rough. "I'm not officially on the auction list, but I'd like to offer myself up anyway."

A stunned silence fell like an anvil, and Fern's stomach dropped with it.

Not because of what he said, but because of *how* he said it. Not with charm. Not with bravado. As if he stood on the edge of a cliff, seconds from plummeting over. Or maybe he'd already fallen.

Trust in destiny?

Fern thought she had, but now, she wasn't so sure.

1

———

August, two years earlier...

*L*ife, Fern knew, didn't always go as planned. But it went in the right direction a lot more often if you helped it along then trusted in destiny.

Basically, that was her go-to plan. Figure out what she wanted, calculate the best route to get there, eliminate the potential problems. That was the part of her agenda that her family and friends knew about.

The final key component, though, was to open her hands and let fate do its thing.

She was delighted to come downstairs at the home she still shared with her parents to discover Grandma Sonora with her mother, the two women enjoying cups of tea at the kitchen table.

"Hey, Granny. You look bright and cheery." Fern dropped

a kiss on her mother Sophie's cheek en route to hugging her grandma.

"Lots to be thankful about," Grandma Sonora informed her, hugging her back with great enthusiasm.

Fern headed for the fridge and the teapot as soon as she was free. "Tell me more, only let me get ready at the same time?"

"Of course." Sonora looked her over as Fern popped bread in the toaster and made her own cup of tea. "You're not wearing your prosthesis today?"

At the table, Sophie snickered into her cup then wiped her face clear of amusement. "Sorry. It's not funny."

"It's totally funny, Mom. Now." Fern sighed and explained further, facing her grandma. "You know my part-time job with the painting company? I was carrying an open paint can, and my attachment jammed. I tried to let go, but the hook didn't open. But since I'd already successfully passed Jimmy three pails, he wasn't expecting an interruption and tugged. Forcefully."

Grandma Sonora looked suitably horrified even as amusement twisted her lips. "This is not going to end well."

"Nope. My prosthesis detached suddenly. Paint flew everywhere. On me and my arm, on him, on the floor, the walls." Fern caught the toast as it popped up. "I have to get it cleaned and repaired."

"Well, you do just fine without it," Sophie pointed out.

"I do, but it's convenient to have." Fern eyed her grandma. "Now tell me more about why you're all lit up with happiness."

"Be careful what you ask for," her mother warned.

"Hush," Grandma Sonora muttered. "Just because the thought of your mother being in love makes you want to slap your hands over your ears, not everyone has the same sensitivities."

Sophie met Fern's gaze, amusement bubbling out of her.

"Tell me, my sweet daughter, do *you* want to listen to your grandma babble on about her sex life?"

"I said *love* life," Sonora protested.

Oh boy. Fern stared at the ceiling, desperately trying to find a proper response that didn't involve breaking into a cackle.

"See? I told you," Sophie said with a laugh.

"She didn't say a word," Grandma Sonora complained.

"She did *the look*. The one Malachi does when all of us are tormenting him and he's trying not to end up in the doghouse after being surrounded by a gaggle of women."

Oops. Fern concentrated on spreading peanut butter to the very edge of her toast. "Thank you for pointing out that tell. I will make sure I avoid it in the future. Grandma Sonora, I am delighted that you are in love. I aspire to be as happy and wholeheartedly head-over-heels as you in my future years. Mother, you and Dad are also very much in love, and very...*demonstrative*...about it. In case you're not aware, sometimes your public conversations lean toward TMI. I can't imagine where you learned it from."

Fern pointedly glanced back and forth between the two older women until they both squirmed slightly, then laughed.

"Fine."

"We'll be good."

Fern straightened and held her toast in the air. "To love."

"To love," they both echoed back.

The older women in her life—and there were a lot of them—always made Fern smile for one reason or another. Her three sisters were just as rock solid as Mom and Grandma, and Fern cherished the moments she got to spend with them.

Her phone rang, and she answered it quickly, hoping she wasn't about to disappoint one of those important people.

"Hey, Rose. Please don't ask me to come in early, because I

can't. I'm going for a trail ride with Tansy and Cody. She's finally cashing in her win from the last bachelor auction."

"That's why I'm calling. Message for you from Tansy. She's sick as a dog."

"Oh no! What's up?" Fern stared out the window, avoiding eye contact with her mom because Sophie was a mind reader at times. One of her babies sick?

She'd be over at the apartment, mothering Tansy within minutes.

"Just a bad summer cold, so she plans to stay in bed today. But—" Rose added before Fern's disappointment could rise, "the trail ride is still on. I called Red Boot ranch and let them know you're still coming out, so go ahead and keep that date."

"Is she sure? We could switch it to another day."

"No. Tansy insists you go," Rose assured her. "Have fun. Tell her all about it when you can. She bid at the auction to mess with people. She wasn't really hoping to date Cody or anything."

Which Fern already knew. "If she's sure..."

"Very sure. Now, I have things to do since I'm the only sister working the café this morning," Rose teased. "Have a blast, and I'll see you this afternoon for your shift."

"Deal. Love you," Fern offered brightly.

"Love you too."

Between catching her mom and grandma up on the details of Tansy's cold and then getting herself ready for the ride, she didn't have time to do more than consider in passing that this wasn't what she'd had in mind when she'd asked to join Tansy and Cody.

She knew him. Sort of. They'd bumped into each other around town over the past few years since he'd moved to Heart Falls, but he was a good bit older than her and didn't run in her usual social circles. She'd met him a few more times recently since his older brother was now dating Rose, but that was the extent of it.

The morning was shaping up to be an entertaining adventure, no matter what happened. Proof once again that she'd done the planning to set up the thing she really wanted—the trail ride—and now it was time to trust in fate.

Whatever it had in store for her.

CODY SWAYED EASILY in the saddle, letting Princess Buttercup pick her own pace down the dusty trail that edged Red Boot's western fence line. It was early enough the high summer heat hadn't set in yet, the sun still polite, and the air tasted faintly of sage and fresh hay.

He'd knocked out chores before dawn to keep the day clear. Fencing check done. Feed delivered. One stubborn calf turned back through the gate it apparently thought was optional.

All so he could ride with Tansy Fields. Too funny.

Princess Buttercup flicked an ear back, annoyed with his drifting mind. He chuckled and adjusted the reins, giving her a reassuring pat on the neck. Smart, steady little mare. Knew the trails better than he did sometimes.

Cody's mind, however, continued to drift. This time to Chance, his older brother who'd come to Heart Falls barely a month ago yet somehow walked right into a life that fit him tighter than a custom saddle.

And Rose Fields. Good Lord, that girl had turned Chance inside out from day one.

"Settled right down, didn't you?" Cody muttered to the horse, but the words were for his brother. He could almost hear Chance's voice in reply, cocky and laughing.

Aye, only feckin' eejits run from a good thing, Cody. Might as well stay put if yer arse likes the bed.

Cody huffed a quiet laugh. Chance's accent always thickened when he got smug, which around Rose was more often than not these days. Not that Cody begrudged either of them the happiness. It was early days yet, but so far the two of them were shaping up to be more than a casual fling.

If Cody was honest with himself, he wouldn't mind a bit of that kind of luck himself. He had steady work, damn good friends, and a stretch of Alberta prairie to live on that felt like home.

Only piece missing was a woman.

He'd found no potential match, though, in the small town of Heart Falls. His halfhearted attempts at love lately had been through an app, and the results were a bunch of ghostings and cat photos. One online hopeful in Nova Scotia was the only one he'd corresponded with more than a few times, and while he enjoyed their conversations, it still felt odd.

They'd been talking about her coming out for a visit, and he was strangely *okay* about it. Which sucked. He should be excited, not simply okay.

Today's ride was supposed to be a break from all that. Tansy was a hoot, and from what Rose had assured him, even though Tansy had bid on Cody at the bachelor auction, she had zero interest in romance.

Perfect. No expectations. No awkwardness. Just a couple hours winding along trails under tall pine trees. Talking about everything and nothing.

As he rounded the last bend to the main arena, Cody pulled Princess Buttercup up short. Parked in the section clearly marked *Visitors* was a beat-up old Ford pickup that definitely hadn't been there at sunrise.

Before he could swing a leg over to dismount, the driver's door flew open and out popped... Not Tansy Fields.

Fern Fields.

He knew her. Sort of. Mostly in the way everyone in Heart Falls knew the Fields family. Salt of the earth and loyal as border collies. They'd met at a few community events, Fern flitting around like a sunbeam. Always smiling. Always moving.

Right now, she bounced on the balls of her feet as if she might launch into orbit. Her curly black hair bobbed in a halo around her head as she moved, the deep tan brown of her skin warm in the morning sunlight.

"Hey, Cody!" she called brightly, waving her bare, short left arm as she approached slowly. No prosthesis today. He'd noticed she wore or didn't wear it with about even timing. He respected that.

"Hey yourself. Where's Tansy?" he asked, scanning behind her as if Tansy might leap from the truck bed with a shout.

Fern stopped a foot away, examining him and the horse with equal interest. "Home, coughing up a lung," she said with a sympathetic grimace. "Rose called and said Tansy's down for the count but insisted I come anyway."

Cody's mouth worked for a second then settled on a slow, careful smile. "So, you and me today, huh?"

Her grin widened, and she rocked back on her heels. "If you don't mind. I promise not to talk your ear off. If you believe that, I have a bridge to sell you."

Something warm trickled through his chest, a quiet spark that made him feel about five years younger.

"I don't mind at all," he said.

It took barely any time to get ready to go as one of the Red Boot ranch hands walked out the big sorrel gelding he'd planned for Tansy to ride.

Cody tied Buttercup to the railing so he could move in to help. "This is Lonesome Charlie. Need a hand up?"

"Please and thank you," Fern said, already stepping close. He caught her waist, warm and slender, and hoisted her up smooth as silk. She settled as if she belonged there, adjusting her reins with easy competence.

Her eyes were so full of mischief it tugged at the edges of his composure. "See? Destiny's helping already. If Tansy was here, I'd have had to haul myself up like a spider monkey."

Cody barked out a laugh. "I somehow doubt you've ever looked awkward in your life."

Her lashes fluttered dramatically. "Flattery from a ranch foreman? Be still my heart."

He watched her a second longer than necessary before clearing his throat. "You look comfy up there. Ride much?"

Fern shot him a pleased smile. "Not as much as I'd like. Our family's been friends with the Stone family since way back, so I used to ride with their youngest son, Dustin. My oldest sister married one of the Stone brothers, and I sneak a ride at Silver Stone at times. But not often enough."

"Well," Cody said, swinging up onto Princess Buttercup beside her, "we'll fix that today."

He led Buttercup forward, careful to keep the horses close but not crowding. Fern adjusted her reins, posture loose and confident. She used the crook of her left arm to pinch the loop while changing the grip on her right. It worked just fine, and Cody relaxed a little more.

Riding always meant being adaptable, and it appeared Fern had things well under control.

"So, Mr. Gabrielle," she said, voice teasing as they set off with the horses at an easy walk. "How's life treating you these days? The ranch looks as if it's still standing. Your brother behaving himself?"

He snorted. "Chance is as happy as a clam, though he'd call me a 'clueless gobshite' if I told him that. Ranch is steady. Bosses are good people. No complaints."

Fern leaned a bit closer. "Any secret ranch gossip to share?"

He snorted. "Wouldn't be a secret long if I told you, now, would it?"

"Fair enough." She hummed under her breath, gaze sweeping the open fields as if she was absorbing every square inch. "I like it out here. Quiet, but not lonely, you know?"

He did. More than he could say without sounding like a sap.

She peeked at him sideways. "So. Since I know your brother and my sister are gaga over each other, it seems I should know this next bit. What about you? Are you seeing anyone special?"

The question was light, playful, but it hit a spot he hadn't expected. Cody considered a moment before answering.

"Seeing someone. Kind of," he admitted. "She's out east. Long-distance thing. Not serious yet, but...we'll see."

He felt rather than saw the shift beside him. Fern's energy didn't dim so much as redirect, pivoting from playful flirt to something brighter and more purely friendly. She laughed lightly, flicking him a grin.

"Well then. Good for you, and good luck. If it's meant to be, I'm sure all the distance in the world won't keep you apart. Destiny doesn't care about your GPS location."

Cody chuckled despite himself.

They rode another hour through the soft rustle of grass and the hush of wind through pine trees. Fern talked about her sisters, her part-time jobs, and her recent graduation from tech design school.

He told her about the horses, the ranch, and was shocked to

find himself mentioning the quiet weight of being the man everyone counted on, even if he didn't say it quite like that.

He deliberately made sure to say nothing about the hollow spot that had been growing in his chest for months. The one her laugh and lilting voice filled, if only for a while.

When they made it back to the arena, Fern swung down on her own with a triumphant little *whoop*, landing lightly in the dust.

"Thanks for letting me steal your morning," she said, patting Lonesome Charlie's flank with a competent ease. "Not what either of us planned, huh?"

"Nope." Cody tied off Buttercup and found himself smiling at her. Really smiling, no half-measures. "But I wouldn't change a thing."

Fern's smile sparkled, wide and certain. "Told you. Destiny always knows what she's doing."

He didn't argue. He didn't dare.

Because maybe destiny really did know best. Which meant maybe he should be fool enough to trust her.

First, though, he had a lot of thinking to do.

2

───────

*F*ern was too busy to ponder the strange sensation she'd experienced that morning out with Cody—

Bullshit.

For the last five days she'd replayed every second of the trail ride so many times in her mind it felt like turning on a favourite movie she could quote line for line. His laugh teased her when she shut her eyes. The way the corner of his mouth tugged up when he was half amused, half baffled by her chatter? She knew it well enough to draw it.

Dangerous territory.

Luckily, Fern Fields was a woman who knew how to steer clear of temptation when necessary.

Well, most of the time.

Right now, she was piloting herself directly to the front door of *Gabrielle's* gallery. She should be tucked in bed instead, but sleep wasn't happening tonight. Not when she'd spent the last hour mentally retracing her final moments at the job and trying to remember if, in her distracted mental state, she'd shut down the very new, very expensive computer she'd been working on.

She'd sworn to Chance she'd lock everything down properly. She'd sworn to herself she'd be the best assistant the new family-run art space could ask for. It wasn't just a paycheck. It was a chance to prove she could wear her organized, professional hat as easily as she wore her life-of-the-party one.

One more step toward wherever destiny nudged her next.

So here she was, on Thursday night just ten minutes shy of midnight, turning her borrowed key in the lock while the Alberta wind nudged her unruly curls across her eyes.

Inside, the gallery was half shadows and half moonlight, the walls lined with carefully hung paintings that made the empty quiet feel alive. She paused, soaking it in for a heartbeat. Even before ever having experienced the low buzz of visitors, a hallowed hush was present that felt as if it deserved respect.

She flicked on the small desk lamp by the front counter then padded down the hall toward the stairwell. Upstairs, she would double-check the computers. Maybe peek at the flyers she'd spent all week tweaking, just to be sure her traitorous brain hadn't added any hint of her wandering thoughts to the pages.

"Focus," she muttered, planting a hand on the railing.

Halfway up, she paused. A low thud and a muffled voice drifted down the stairwell. She held her breath, tilting her head to listen.

Another thud. A string of hushed curses. Definitely familiar curses. The Irish lilt was already far too familiar.

Fern grinned despite herself. "Should've known."

She pushed the door open to the second-floor studio and stepped into a warm pocket of light and cluttered genius. Brushes, open tubes of paint, empty mugs, and at the center of it all, Chance Gabrielle, perched barefoot on a stool, his shirt covered in a wild variety of green and blue paints.

He didn't even notice her at first. He muttered something in Irish, stabbed at the canvas with a paintbrush, then sighed so hard his shoulders slumped.

"Don't mind me," Fern said softly. "Just your friendly neighbourhood office fairy come to shut things down before your computer runs away screaming."

Chance turned, bleary-eyed as he blinked hard. "I thought you'd gone home hours ago."

"I did. Came back." She pointed at his paint brush. "Careful, that thing's loaded."

He swore again, tipping the brush into a plastic yogurt container. "Don't look, okay? It's not ready."

Fern snorted. "Of course I won't look, but I'm not sure why you're *desperation painting* in the middle of the night when you have only a short time to go until the gallery opening."

"It'll make sense," he promised before making a face at the canvas she couldn't see. "Gods, I hope it'll make sense."

"It will," Fern assured him. "Now drink water and focus. I'll be gone in no time."

She gave him a playful salute and carefully avoided peeking as she slipped past him into the open office space.

The computers were all shut down properly, because of course they were. She made a mental note to get Chance to invest in an automatic backup service, then left herself a sticky note on the monitor. *Take picture end of day of all systems off.*

Ten minutes later, she'd made a few final notes for the upcoming opening, flicked off the lamp, and tiptoed back through the studio. She meant to ghost right out, but a familiar deep hum rumbled softly from the front corner.

Cody.

Fern froze mid-step. He leaned on the window frame,

staring out at the night through the big glass windows that looked out onto Main Street. He stood like he'd been carved from moonlight. Sharp jaw, eyes bright as he hummed softly.

For a heartbeat, Fern considered backing out the way she'd come. Then he turned, catching her in the act.

She lifted her fingers in a sheepish wave. "Hey, cowboy."

Cody pushed to vertical, a slow smile pulling at his mouth. "Hey yourself. You break in?"

"I'm on the payroll, thank you very much. Just doing an overly diligent job. What's your excuse for the midnight stroll?" As he walked closer, Fern caught a whiff of soap and coffee and a hint of roast beef.

He pointed to a basket on the front counter that held a thermos and something wrapped in brown paper. "Making sure my brother doesn't forget he's human. I'll feed him then offer to tie him to a chair if he doesn't sleep."

"Good plan. He'd probably fight you, though."

"Oh, he has," Cody said dryly. "He threatened to paint my truck pink if I nagged him again."

Fern snickered, picturing his lovely deep blue truck in bubble-gum pink. Maybe that was why she didn't notice she'd stepped closer, nearly toe-to-toe with him now, shadows and lamplight wrapping them in a quiet little cave.

His eyes held hers for a moment too long. Then he exhaled, voice going softer. "Broke things off."

It was ridiculous how quickly she figured out just what the heck he was talking about. Her heart did a slow, traitorous flip. "With your East Coast sweetie?"

"Yeah. Few nights back. After Chance's art night with the guys, I..." He trailed off, scrubbing a hand over his mouth. "It wasn't fair to her. Or me. Or—" He didn't finish the sentence. He didn't need to.

Fern swallowed hard and tried for breezy. "Sounds as if you

gave it some serious thought. Good for you, cowboy, for making a tough decision. To be honest, long-distance love affairs have always sounded like real killers."

He huffed a laugh, low and rueful. "Yeah."

Silence settled between them, not heavy, but not light either. It lingered in her ribs, in the stubborn way her pulse tapped out a Morse code message she refused to translate.

"Look at us. Both here being painfully responsible," she said, nudging him lightly with her shoulder. "How about I'll double-check the back door then leave out the front. You can go try to move Chance, but we both know he's not leaving tonight."

A grin tugged at his lips. "True, he's not."

For a heartbeat, the air between them buzzed with something unspoken. Cody's gaze dropped to her mouth, then back to her eyes, like he might say something reckless.

Fern cleared her throat and lifted her chin. "I'm really glad that we're friends," she said firmly before he could tempt her common sense away.

A crooked smile tugged at his lips. He tilted his head, conceding. "Friends."

She gave him a mock salute, stepping back before she could change her mind. "Now, go shoo Chance off his stool."

His fingers brushed her arm. Brief, warm, and enough to scatter every plan she'd just reinforced like startled birds.

Then he was gone, boots thudding softly up the stairs. Fern stayed where she was for one breath, two, hand pressed over her chest.

Destiny needed to lay off and wait.

Cody dealt with his brother then headed home to the ranch. He stepped into the warm prairie night and immediately wanted to punch the nearest fence post.

Smooth, Gabrielle. Real smooth. Blurting out he'd broken things off with his "East Coast sweetie" like a lovesick teenager fishing for a reaction. Agreeing—again very foolishly—to Fern's easy *friends* declaration before he'd even figured out what he wanted.

Not that wanting anything with Fern Fields was smart. Or fair. She was bright, ambitious, and so, *so* young. On top of that, with the thing developing between Chance and Rose, did he have a right to do anything that might mess up his brother's hopes for a future?

No. Time to lay off and be grateful for the reminder of being friends only.

Still. Her laugh stuck like opportunistic burrs, teasing him at all moments of the day and night. The worst part? He liked the repetitive prodding. Far too much.

A week before the grand opening, anticipation buzzed through the gallery louder than a hornet's nest. Chance was all but living there, high on paint fumes and love. Whatever had gone down with Rose a day or two earlier had put a permanent grin on Cody's brother's face, but Chance's brain was still a jumbled mess.

Which meant Cody spent half his time keeping things rolling at Red Boot ranch, half playing gopher between the ranch and the gallery, and all of it trying not to think about the curve of Fern Fields's grin when she teased him.

Late on the seventeenth, only nights before the opening, Cody packed up the box of expensive equipment Chance had left at the ranch for safe keeping and hauled it back into town, grumbling under his breath the whole way.

The gallery was locked for the night, but the lights upstairs were still burning. He knew who that meant.

He found her exactly where he expected, in the interactive studio. What he didn't expect was to find her tussling with a wheeled display cabinet almost her size. She wore cut-offs and a soft blue tank top, curly hair loose and natural.

She looked like trouble wrapped in summer.

"Hold up there, Hercules," he called. "You planning to move that alone?"

Fern jumped. "Cody! You scared the hell out of me."

He made his way to her side. "You're going to break your pretty neck if you tip that thing."

She stuck out her tongue before turning on the charm. "It needs to be moved for tomorrow's soft opening. I thought I could muscle it around. But now that you're here, you can do it for me."

He sighed dramatically. "Step aside, bossypants."

They got the cabinet rolling easy enough until it snagged on a loose loop of extension cord near the VR corner. Fern bent to shove while Cody braced the far end. She gave one good push, lost her footing, and toppled against him.

Vanilla and lavender danced off her skin, filling his head with really bad ideas. If he followed up on his instincts, he'd do something truly unwise right this second.

He looked down. She looked up. Her lips parted.

Cody kissed her.

It was a reckless kiss. Not practiced, not gentle. It was a hard, sudden press of mouths that cracked something inside him wide open.

She made a startled noise then curled her fingers in his shirt and kissed him right back, fierce and soft all at once.

It could have gone further. Should have, maybe. But beside

them, the cabinet shifted again, pushing tighter into Cody's hip.

She broke the kiss on a half laugh-half gasp. "It's alive!"

He laughed too, breathless and hoarse. "Hold still—"

They wrangled the beast back onto level flooring. Fern brushed a loose ringlet back from her right cheek, still grinning as if they hadn't just exploded the friends agreement.

But then she stepped back.

Not far. Just enough.

"Cody..." she began.

He knew that tone. He hated that he knew it so well. "Yeah?"

She hummed softly for a second, her eyes clear and bright despite the flush on her cheeks. "I like you. A lot."

"Good." His voice came out rough. He wanted to pull her back in, kiss her until all the common sense drained from both their heads.

She didn't move. "But I'm not looking for a boyfriend."

His brow furrowed. "Oh?"

"I bet you'd make a *great* boyfriend." Her mouth curved up, but her eyes stayed serious. "But not for me, not right now. Not while I'm still sorting stuff out." She shrugged, the motion light as air yet heavy as stone. "If it's meant to be, it'll happen. Just... not now."

He swallowed hard. Part of him wanted to argue. To promise he'd make it feel right. Hell, he wanted to seduce her until she couldn't remember why waiting seemed so smart.

Instead, he pressed his forehead to hers in a quiet surrender. "Friends until the time's right?"

"Friends until the time's right," Fern agreed.

～

Just over a week later, Cody stepped into the upper level of the gallery, half-wishing he'd skipped the tie. He tugged at it now, the silk a noose that didn't belong around a man's throat, especially not when his heart was already climbing up there to fight for air.

He'd come to support Chance, no question about that. His brother deserved every ounce of respect tonight for pulling off this mad, brilliant show. Cody might have carried sandwiches and coffee and a hundred complaints up these stairs for weeks, but Chance had bled his heart for Rose Fields out onto canvas, and the result was glorious.

So he'd stand there, in his monkey suit, and pretend everything felt normal.

Except it didn't.

Because behind all the laughter and polite applause, somewhere in this maze of paint and pixels, Fern Fields was making him forget how to breathe.

Chance spotted him first. "Alright, brother? This way."

Cody forced a grin, lifted his hand in a lazy wave. "Sorry I'm late, but it looks as if it's been a success so far."

"It's gone well." Chance gave him a once-over. "You're in a suit."

Cody adjusted the knot under his throat, trying not to scratch at it like a farm dog with fleas. "Figured it was the least I could do."

"You fed me while I painted so that I wouldn't starve. That was above and beyond the line of duty as far as I'm concerned." Chance's voice carried more than gratitude. Pride too. Cody would bottle that if he could.

He huffed. "Thanks. But next time, feed yourself. I don't want to have to wear this to your funeral."

"But you'd look dashing. There is that."

Cody rolled his eyes, the easy banter pulling him halfway back to calm. "Take better care of yourself."

"I intend to. And of Rose."

Cody followed Chance's line of sight, and there she was, Rose Fields, the reason Chance had painted like a man possessed. Beside her, her sister Tansy. The tight-knit love of family clear in their body language.

Cody's chest tightened before his mind caught up. *Family*, his brain repeated helpfully, even as another name—*Fern*—threaded through every thought and sent a low hum under his ribs.

His brother caught him drifting, so Cody raised his head sharply. He tilted it to indicate Rose. "You two are well suited. Don't fuck this up."

"You can't mess up destiny," Chance said.

The drop of the word *destiny* hit hard.

"That's what I said."

Fern. He hadn't even seen her slip around the corner. Now she stood there, bright as a star, so effortlessly herself that the floor shifted under his polished shoes.

"Right, Cody?"

He nearly tripped over empty air, scrambling to plant his boots before he made a complete fool of himself. *Steady, cowboy. You agreed. Friends. She asked for space. She deserves your word to mean something.*

"Fern." He offered a quick chin dip.

She cocked her head, mischief dancing in her eyes as she examined his suit. "That's a good look on you. But so's your cowboy gear."

Heat crawled up the back of his neck. He opened his mouth. Shut it. Opened it again. *Say something normal. Something smart. Or just—go. Before you step over there and kiss her silly.*

He coughed, focused on Chance instead. "I'm going downstairs to take another peek at the show. Great job. Catch up with you tomorrow. Fern, we'll see you 'round."

It was the best he could do. Run before he forgot how.

He pivoted fast enough to dodge Rose and Tansy's curious eyes, boots hitting the polished floor with more force than grace.

Don't turn back, he ordered himself. *Let her laugh. Let her tease you about fate. You'll keep your word. Friends. Nothing more, yet. But someday...*

Behind him, Fern's voice chased him down the stairs, smug and sweet and sure of things he wasn't ready to claim. "Cody? Running from fate. Skipping out on destiny. Something like that."

Cody nearly laughed out loud, totally amused at their inside joke. *Yeah, sweetheart. Something like that.*

For now, he let himself hope destiny wouldn't wait too long.

3

———

September, one year later…

Cody had thought life after the kiss, and committing to be only friends, would get…well, more awkward for one thing. Pushing aside the attraction between them should have seemed wrong or forced.

But it hadn't.

If anything, interactions between them felt exactly how they should: easy, steady, real.

He still thought Fern Fields was the most attractive woman he'd ever seen, but instead of that truth ruining things, it had settled somewhere deep inside him. Every time they bumped shoulders at a family barbecue, or when she leaned in close at a Fields kitchen table full of gossip and leftover pie, it just made him want to know her more.

And he did. Piece by piece, laugh by laugh, truth by stubborn, warm-hearted truth.

No drama. No crossing lines. Just two people learning to be friends.

Until today.

Tonight, to be exact.

If anyone asked him later, Cody Gabrielle would blame it entirely on that damned ringlet of hair she'd left loose on purpose—or fate had—because every time she tilted her head, that dark curl bounced and twirled like a hypnotist's watch, telling him *forget every promise and taste her one more time.*

He dragged his gaze back to his half-empty beer, willing his brain to remember all the reasons kissing Fern was a bad idea.

Rough Cut Pub was full tonight with ranch crews off shift and locals mixing it up with out-of-towners. Chance and Rose were tangled together on the dance floor as if the world didn't exist beyond each other.

From a booth on the far side of the room, Tansy waved but her focus remained tight on the two female friends at her side.

Cody was having an okay evening, that bouncy curl aside, until he caught sight of Shim, the clean-cut Silver Stone ranch hand with the polite manners and too-handsome smile, spinning Fern in a lazy two-step under the string lights.

Cody sipped his beer, slow and deliberate. *Accidents happened all the time on ranches,* he reminded himself. *Fence posts fall, horses spook, guys named Shim find themselves face-first in horse shit.*

Fern laughed, full and bright, and Shim's grin widened as if he thought he had a chance in hell.

Cody swallowed down a growl and focused on the last of his beer.

Before he could plot any more suspicious barn mishaps for the guy, which was a total waste of time considering Shim worked at Silver Stone and not Red Boot, Fern spun away from the young man and beelined for Cody, her gaze locked on his.

Her sunshine yellow dress paired with cowboy boots that showed off her legs to perfection. Tonight she wore her prothesis, the midnight black and silver section on her left arm glittering in the dance floor lights.

He didn't move. Couldn't have if he'd tried.

"Hey there, cowboy," she teased, breathless from dancing, cheeks flushed a soft rose that did bad things to his pulse. "Why are you brooding over here like a tragic hero when there's good music playing?"

"I'm not brooding," he lied.

Her eyes sparkled with wicked delight as she grabbed his hand. "Liar. Come on."

She tugged him up, no protest possible, and dragged him right into the press of bodies swaying to the next song. Before he knew it, she'd laid her left arm lightly over his right, her right hand resting on his chest right where his heartbeat threatened to give him away.

"Happy?" he murmured, dipping his head to catch her words over the music.

She hummed a yes and leaned in. "Very."

They moved together, easy as breathing. She smelled like summer and soap and a hint of the spiced cider she'd been drinking. Cody breathed deep, soaking in her scent.

"Work going okay?" she asked, lifting her chin so her eyes caught his in the shifting light.

"Busy. Bookings scheduled into the New Year. My bosses have threatened to hire more hands for me to wrangle." He smirked. "Poor souls."

Fern laughed, and all her dark ringlets bounced, catching the light like blue-black diamonds and torturing him all over again. "You'll make a lovely tyrant."

"And you? Gallery still your kingdom?"

"Always." Her smile widened, triumphant. "Chance keeps trying to boss me. I let him pretend it works."

"You could run the entire county if you wanted, Fern Fields."

She tilted her head, mock serious. "I probably could if I wanted to. Now to figure out if that's what would really make me happy."

Before he could tease her back, something failed in Rough Cut's electrical system. A loud *pop* sang from the speakers right before sudden darkness swallowed them. Even the dim red of the exit signs flickered out.

As the crowd gasped, then half laughed and half complained, Cody's protective instincts roared to life. His arm slid around Fern's back, pulling her in tighter before she could so much as blink.

"You okay?" His voice rumbled against her hair.

She pressed her cheek to his chest, voice muffled but teasing. "Kicking into hero mode, are you? It's just the power, cowboy."

"Don't care." He shifted them sideways as people fumbled for phones. "Stay close."

She did. Too close. Perfectly close.

His hand found hers as they navigated the dance floor through the press of bodies as confused laughter rang out. In the soft glow from his phone flashlight, he caught a flash of her face. Reckless, trusting, lit from inside.

Outside the pub, the night was a wash of cool air and scattered stars. The sudden hush after the music and loud noises made his pulse roar in his ears.

Fern squeezed his hand once, her lips parting as if to say something clever.

Destiny...

He didn't let her finish.

Cody cupped her cheek with his free hand, brushed his thumb against her warm skin, and kissed her.

Softly first. So soft. A question and a confession all in one. She sighed into him, and that tiny sound broke whatever restraint he had left. He slanted his mouth harder, deeper, tasting her laugh, her quiet gasp, her everything.

They staggered sideways to the edge of the back alley, half-shielded by the pub's shadowed siding, lost in the kind of kiss that made ignoring the world easy. Her right hand fisted his shirt, tugging him closer, closer, until all his carefully built walls gave way.

His brain spun in useless circles. Apologies, excuses, plans, but none of it mattered. Fern's mouth was warm and sweet, and she was right there, kissing him as if she'd waited an entire year for this as well.

Friends, huh?

Destiny, that patient witch, had finally had another idea.

He kissed her as if she was the only thing tethering him to the earth.

And Fern...

Well, hell. She wasn't about to stop him.

Her mind, usually so quick to sort and categorize and plan, went deliciously blank. All she knew was the warmth of his hands, the rough brush of stubble when he angled closer. The taste of him with hints of beer and the fresh air he always carried with him, like wide-open prairie and safety.

When he finally pulled back, both of them breathless, she stayed right there. His forehead rested lightly on hers, and his smile was broad, the feel of his kiss echoing through her.

"Hi," she whispered, inanely giddy.

"Hey yourself," he murmured back, brushing her cheekbone again.

God, she'd wanted this, wanted *him*, for so long...

And yet not at all.

Because she'd meant what she'd told him all that time ago. She hadn't wanted a boyfriend just to fill a space. She'd needed to build the rest of her life first, to stand on ground that was solidly hers.

Now she thought she had.

Her job at the art gallery wasn't just because of a favour being done by a doting sweetheart for a family member. It was *hers*. The high-tech wings, the digital showcases, the community events and full-to-the-brim calendar. She'd dreamed them up and made them real.

Chance might be the artist with the worldwide connections, but Fern Fields had become his secret weapon, the glue behind every successful show.

She was twenty-three, nearly the age she'd scribbled on her childhood goal chart under 'Find my forever person'. She'd laughed when she found the old tattered journal last month, the one filled with her childish and not so childish dreams all laid out in multicoloured glitter pen glory.

Deep down, wanting this now felt right.

Her friends were moving forward too. Charity was engaged to Dustin, planning a wedding full of family celebrations and laughter. Fern was so happy for them it made her chest ache.

Yet sometimes being the last Fields sister at home felt exactly like being last picked at recess.

She wanted someone to hold her hand. To kiss her like Cody just had. As if the world might disappear if he didn't.

Her heart fluttered hard as he traced his thumb along her jaw again. He looked as if he might say something serious.

"You know," she teased softly, "I always thought destiny was stubborn, but this is a record, even for her."

He laughed, warm and low. "Couldn't avoid it forever."

She tapped her fingers on his chest. "So. Now what?"

Cody drew back just enough to look at her properly. Even in the faint glow from the pub's window, the wicked glint in his eyes flashed at her and did dangerous things to her resolve.

"Now," he said, voice firm and gentle at once, "I'm going to take you out."

Fern blinked. "Take me out. Like a date?"

"Yeah, darlin'. A real date. Something more than me pressing you up against a wall outside a bar."

Heat flared in her cheeks but she couldn't stop smiling. "Hmm. The date sounds suspiciously wholesome."

He chuckled, leaned in to nip at her lower lip. A quick taste that made her toes curl inside her boots. "Doesn't have to be *too* wholesome. That's up to you."

If anything, Fern flushed harder. But that too was a good thing to know. "What's the agenda for the date?"

"You'll find out when it happens." Cody eyed her earnestly. "I want to surprise you."

"Oh?" She poked a finger into his chest, making a face as she considered. "Okay, fine. But can this surprise involve horses?"

"It can. It will," he promised. "You still off both Mondays and Tuesdays?"

"Mm-hmm." Because after a year of being friends, they knew each other's schedules and so much more.

"Good. Tuesday morning. Be ready."

She arched a brow. "How ready are we talking? Lip gloss and out on the town ready, or full-on field work ready?"

He grinned, teeth flashing white. "Somewhere in between. But dress warm. I'll pick you up at seven."

Fern's jaw dropped before she could stop it. "Seven? In the *morning?*"

His lips quirked, mischief in his eyes. "I can make it six."

She smacked his chest lightly, earning another quiet laugh that made her insides flutter all over again. God help her. She was so ready to fall fast.

He glanced past her shoulder, and she followed his gaze. The power was back on, and lights danced onto the sidewalk and street through the open doors of the pub as people returned to the floor.

All of them oblivious to the world-shifting moment that just happened in the shadows outside, Fern thought with amusement.

Her friends would be...

Her family...

Oh dear.

She groaned under her breath before offering Cody the brightest expression she could muster. "What do you say to the idea that we keep this to ourselves for a little while?"

He hesitated, smile fading slightly. "You don't want people to know we're dating?"

She hurried to reassure him. "Not because I want to hide —" Fern stopped dead. She wasn't about to lie, and secrecy was exactly what she was hoping for. "No, I really *do* want to hide this from everyone, just for a little while." She met his gaze straight on. "I have a very large and loving family who like to meddle. This thing between us, it feels special. I want to keep it between us for as long as we can."

Thank God, Cody laughed. "With less interference from your sisters and my brother?"

"And my parents, and grandparents, and Charity and her fiancé. Your bosses, and their sisters, and your coworkers..."

He whistled softly. "The list is long, isn't it?"

"It means we both have lots of people in our lives who love us. That's the good part," Fern affirmed even as she wrinkled her nose, slightly frustrated by the simple truth. "I adore them all and they really are a pain in the butt at times."

"I hear you," Cody assured her. His expression went thoughtful, eyes turned toward the starry sky. Then he nodded, meeting her gaze again. "I won't lie if I'm asked a direct question, but it could be fun to see how long it takes for anyone to figure out what's going on."

"Exactly." Fern tapped his chest again. "*We* know we're dating, but until asked, we wait to see who notices."

His conspiratorial wink made something inside her ache in a good way for an entirely different reason. It wasn't just a physical attraction between them. Not anymore. The little connections that had built over the past year were there like support beams, turning even a small secret more meaningful.

It was *theirs,* and that made it important.

"*Fern.*" From the top of the boardwalk, Charity waved.

Fern waved back then turned to Cody. "See you Tuesday."

"You bet. Now go before I kiss you again and blow our cover wide open before we've even begun."

She raised a brow and considered. "Depending on the kiss, it might be worth it."

He laughed, pushing her gently toward the door.

Charity waited for her in the light of the doorway, heels bouncing lightly to the music. "You okay? That blackout was wild for a few minutes."

"I'm fine. You guys?"

"Better than fine. Dustin hauled me off the floor and we entertained ourselves in the dark, no problem." Charity grinned and Fern offered the expected eye roll and held her secret in tightly.

Her mind was already slipping away to the future. To surprises and a sweet and sexy cowboy with mischief in his eyes.

4

———————

Fern hurried down the stairs and slid into the front foyer three minutes before Cody was supposed to arrive. Partly because she'd taken longer to get ready than expected, changing outfits more times than she should have, and partly to avoid meeting one of her parents.

She and Cody had said they wouldn't lie to direct questions about what they were doing, but keeping her mouth shut would be the simplest way to keep things *hush hush* for at least a week.

She shoved her feet into her boots, pulled her coat off the rack—

"You're up early on your day off." Sophie stood in the archway leading to the family room, hands wrapped around a mug of tea.

"Off for an adventure," Fern tossed out. Generic, yet reason enough to excuse her odd behaviour.

"Nice," her mom said. She stepped to the window beside the door and peered out. "That's Cody's truck."

"Yup." Fern slipped her coat on and reached for the doorknob.

Her mom beat her to it, swinging the door open and offering a kiss goodbye. "Say hello to Chance and Rose from me." Sophie waved at the truck.

"Okay." Fern scurried away so fast she was all the way down the sidewalk before Cody could make it around the truck to open the passenger door for her.

He waved back at the house as she crawled in then returned to the driver's seat before eyeing her cautiously. "Is our secret gone that quickly?"

"No." Fern let the wave of shock pass by before amusement snuck in. She turned to face Cody. "Mom saw you and assumed we were meeting up with Rose and Chance."

"Sweet." Cody put the truck in gear and pulled away from the curb. "Let's not hang around and wait for your dad to come out with something for us to deliver to one of them."

He drove toward Red Boot ranch, and for a hopeful moment Fern imagined they were headed to grab horses.

Instead, he took them on an old forestry road that twisted high into the foothills, and not even Cody's sturdy old blue Ford could eliminate the bumping and rattling beneath them.

Fern braced herself to stop from bouncing too far. Her breath kept catching every time he shot her that sideways grin. The one that crinkled the corners of his eyes and made her stomach swoop as if they'd hit a hidden pothole.

Although on this road, it was up in the air which was the actual cause of the butterflies in her belly.

"Question," she said brightly, gripping the edge of her seat as they bobbed over another rut. "Should I be worried you're driving me this far from civilization?"

Cody snorted. "Trust me, sweetheart. If I wanted to hide your body, there are spots closer to home."

"Comforting," Fern deadpanned.

She let her head fall back against the seat and watched the

early sunlight flicker through the tall pines overhead. Temperatures were crisp at this elevation, cool enough if she leaned toward the window, she thought it might fog up.

When he turned off the main gravel onto an even narrower track, Fern raised an eyebrow. "This is an official road, right?"

"Define *official*."

"Does it appear on a map?"

"Maybe a *very* old one."

Fern bit back a laugh as the truck lurched and rocked its way through the underbrush, branches whispering across the windows. "You're the worst tour guide ever."

"Funny, because I haven't heard you ask to turn back yet."

She didn't, either.

When the trees finally parted, opening to a small meadow ringed by rocks and stubby spruce, Cody killed the engine then reached behind the seat to grab a battered old knapsack.

"Come on," he said, grinning at her. "Don't look so suspicious. Five-minute walk. I promise it's worth it."

They clambered out, boots crunching over dry pine cones and loose needles. Fern tugged her coat tighter. The early morning mountain air had a bite to it, but the sunshine made it sparkle too.

She followed him up a faint game trail, half tripping when he turned to catch her hand and tug her up the last rocky rise.

Then she saw them.

Below the ridge, a shallow, winding stream cut through a wide clearing dotted with wild rose bushes and bleached logs. On the far side, grazing calmly, were horses.

Not ranch stock. Not branded. Lean, shaggy creatures with long manes and wary eyes that lifted as she and Cody paused, still as fence posts.

Fern's breath caught so hard it burned. "Are they—"

"Wild?" Cody murmured, his voice soft against her temple.

"Yeah. Or feral, technically. Been a few bands roaming these foothills forever. They stay up here if they've got enough grass. They gave us grief a few years ago, drifting onto Red Boot land. They've been staying on their side of the fence since then, so now it's a pleasure to see them."

Fern pressed a hand over her mouth, like the awe might spill out too loudly if she didn't. Below, a black mare flicked her tail and nudged a bright bay foal closer to her side.

"They're beautiful," Fern whispered.

"Figured you'd think so." Cody's arm slid around her waist, anchoring her when her knees went a little soft. "Found them two weeks ago when I came up hunting strays."

She turned in his arms just enough to catch his grin. "You brought me here to see *this*?"

"Yup."

"Cody, this is..." She searched for the word. Found it lodged somewhere deep and soft in her chest. "Perfect."

He didn't say anything right away. Just brushed his thumb under her chin, tipping her face up so he could kiss her. Slow this time, lazy and thorough. The kind of kiss that made the cool air and distant mountains and his warm jacket pressed to her all blur into one huge sensation.

When he pulled back, Fern tugged him down again to steal one more, laughing into his mouth when he chuckled against her lips.

"Keep that up and they'll run for sure," he teased.

"Sorry," she murmured, completely unrepentant. She pressed her forehead to his. "Not sorry."

They found a dry spot on an old log a few minutes later, close enough to keep watching the little herd but far enough away that the horses settled down and mostly ignored them.

Cody dug out a thermos, and using the cap as a travel mug,

he poured them a cup of strong, black coffee. "I forgot the extra cup, so we'll have to share."

Fern wrinkled her nose. "Thanks?"

He snickered then pulled out a Ziplock baggie full of sugar cubes. "I know how you take your coffee. That sweet tooth of yours is going to be the death of me. But have at 'er."

Shoulders brushing, they passed the cup between them, whispering and pointing out which horses were their favourites.

Somewhere in that quiet, Fern realized her heart wasn't racing from the sight of the wild horses anymore. It buzzed with how natural this felt. How right.

She nudged his boot with hers. "We should lay a wager. On how long we can keep our secret going. About us seeing each other."

"After this morning and your mom's easy assumptions?" Cody leaned back, balancing on his elbows, squinting at her with that lazy affection she was quickly becoming addicted to. "I'm going to go with months. Like...mid-December."

"Optimist. I like that about you." She pretended to think, winding a ringlet around her finger. "If we make it to the end of September, I'll be happily shocked."

"There's the bet." His grin turned wolfish. "Now we need to haggle over the wager."

She acted as if maidenly offended. "You don't want to simply enjoy bragging rights? I'm shocked, Mr. Gabrielle."

"I'm a nice guy, but not that nice," he teased. He tipped his hat down to shade his eyes then pulled her in until her head rested on his chest.

As they inclined into each other, awareness of him grew intensely. The strength in the long length of his muscular body, the firm grip of his arm wrapped around her.

The steady thump of his heart under her cheek.

"I like this," she murmured. "Us. Not having to pretend we're just friends anymore."

"Me too, sweetheart," he rumbled, low and content

She smiled against his jacket. *The secret. The horses. Him.* All of it hers. For now.

Hopefully for at least another week.

CODY GOT Fern home just before noon, easing the truck along her quiet street like a man with nothing to hide. Inside, he still hummed with the echo of her laughter and the way she'd curled up under his arm while the horses grazed below.

He'd packed her a picnic breakfast. He'd fed her sugar-laced coffee and stolen half a dozen kisses under that big Alberta sky. They'd made a memory.

It was a start, yet driving away felt as if he were leaving something half finished. He didn't want to get greedy, but every part of him already craved the next stolen hour.

Back at Red Boot, a soft breeze carried the scent of cut hay from the nearby fields, warm from the sun but with that early hint of autumn threading through as well. Somewhere down by the corrals, a couple of mares nickered lazily. Someone, probably old Bert, was whistling off-key, the ranch hand a stubborn ghost in his seventies who refused to retire.

The main yard stretched wide and open, framed by the jagged rise of the Rockies in the distance. On days like this, Cody never felt boxed in. The land gave him room to think, to breathe, to be useful in ways that mattered.

A clatter by the row of guest cottages snapped him back. Two of the hired hands, Austin and Grant, stood beside a window frame, arguing about the caulking gun.

Austin spotted him first, waving to get his attention. "Boss! You got a sec?"

Cody angled his hat back and sauntered over, gravel crunching under his boots. "Looking for more work?"

Grant barked a laugh, raising both hands in surrender. "We already found plenty to add to the list you gave us. We're working on the pre-winter check lists on the cabins, and turns out, a few of the window casings are pretty shot. They're not old enough to have this kind of wear and tear."

"Good catch. That's the kind of damage that could turn this place into an icebox come January." Cody squinted at the peeling paint and the warping edges catching the sunlight. "These cabins were built only four years ago, so the windows will still be under warranty. I'll check the file."

Austin wiped sweat off his brow with his sleeve. "We'll finish all the cabins right now so we know how many you need to get on their case about."

"Perfect." Cody gave Grant an approving smack on the shoulder. "Better to have to fix this now and not when it means freezing our asses off. First round is on me the next time we hit Rough Cut."

Both young men puffed up their chests. Grant ducked back inside to measure the sill. Austin lingered, toeing the gravel as if he wanted to say more.

"Something else?" Cody asked.

"Uh...not really. Just, uh—" Austin scratched behind his ear. "That pretty gal, Fern. The one working for your brother? She's real nice. Helped my sister out when she visited the gallery last month. Fern made Lindzie feel all fancy and important, and not silly at all for not knowing the fancy words for art stuff."

Cody schooled his face carefully. "Fern is good people, that's for sure."

"You see her sometime, you tell her I said thanks." Austin hustled after Grant, still rattling off items left on their to-do list.

Cody watched them a moment longer, the warmth in his chest strong as the quiet hum of the ranch wrapped back around him. A good day's work made the world small and manageable. Fence posts, horses, fresh paint. Things he could fix.

Inside the barn, the scent of clean straw and old cedar hit him like a balm. Marigold greeted him with that soft, dusty whicker, her long ears swiveling forward as he clicked his tongue.

"Hey there, pretty girl," he murmured, running knuckles along the warm velvet of her cheek. "Heard you were favouring your back leg. Let's see."

She shifted obligingly, leaning her big head into his chest as if to apologize for being trouble. He braced his hand on the latch, mind half on the swelling he expected to find—and his fingers hesitated.

A tiny pause. No more.

Barely enough to catch his attention before it passed. The latch lifted. Marigold's breath puffed over his collarbone, warm and sweet.

"Sorry. Just being a clumsy old man," he told her softly. He checked the joint. Just a bit puffy, probably a stone bruise or mild strain. He'd cold hose it this afternoon, an easy fix.

Outside by the feed shed, he leaned into a sun-warmed post, pulling out his phone with deliberate care to respond to the ping of an incoming message.

Chance: Hey, wee brother. Got a minute?

His thumb hovered an extra second over the keys before he typed.

> Cody: Of course. What's up? Run out of paint?

> Chance: Eejit. Rose says to remind you about Friday night. Dinner here then game night. Fern is coming, and Luke and Kelli. Don't say no. I.e., you can't say no because she's already planned the teams and your presence is required. Don't know why, but for some reason, she likes you. Arse.

Cody huffed out a quiet laugh that startled the barn swallows from the eaves. *Gobshite*, Chance would've called him in person. His older brother had an Irish tongue sharper than any fence staple when he chose to.

Luke and Kelli were solid friends from the community.

And Fern. Her knees bumping his under the table, her eyes saying *later* in a way that made their secret taste even sweeter.

> Cody: Wouldn't miss it. Need me to bring anything?

> Chance: Just your ugly mug. See you then, foreman.

Cody pocketed the phone, pushed away from the fence, and let his gaze roam over the spread he called home. Past the tidy barns, the gleaming metal roofs catching sunlight, out toward the distant roll of pines marching past the foothills and halfway up the mountains.

A good day's work behind him. A mare to check at sunset. A secret date to plan that was even better than wild horses and sugar cubes.

The odd echo in his hand was already fading from memory.

5

———————

ose's kitchen smelled like comfort. Cinnamon from an apple crisp cooled by the window, garlic butter from Chance's over-the-top garlic knots. The faintest undercurrent of paint and turpentine that always clung to her big sister's life now.

Fern leaned her hip against the counter, listening to Luke Stone explain some new fencing plan to Chance, while his wife Kelli sat perched on a barstool, one hand absently rubbing her belly.

Seventeen weeks pregnant. Fern still couldn't wrap her head around it. A baby. A *person*, growing right there inside Kelli.

The concept wasn't the problem, obviously, it was just that no one in Fern's immediate family had ever been pregnant.

It was a fascinating thing to think about and observe.

Kelli's eyes suddenly went wide. Her hand stilled, and her mouth formed a tiny *oh*.

"You okay?" Fern asked quickly, stepping closer.

Kelli's smile was pure wonder. "The baby moved. Just once, but—*wow*."

Fern squealed under her breath. She squeezed Kelli's shoulder, and a pang of something soft and greedy twisted low in her belly. *Someday. Not now, but someday.* Maybe a baby with dark eyes that crinkled like Cody's did when he smiled.

Fern stuffed the daydream away before she lit up like a neon sign.

Instead, she swiped a slice of cheese off Chance's charcuterie board, ignoring his fake outrage.

"Oi! Grab a plate, ya heathen."

"Too slow, big brother," Fern shot back then popped the cheese in her mouth before beaming at Rose for backup.

Rose rolled her eyes fondly and went back to mixing the salad.

Behind her, Cody's quiet chuckle shivered straight up Fern's spine. She risked a peek. He stood near the fridge, beer in hand, nodding at the conversation while his eyes, those traitorous, secret-keeping eyes, kept drifting to her.

Fern crossed her arms, fighting amusement. *Behave,* she mouthed at him.

He lifted his brows and mouthed back, *Make me.*

Heaven help her.

Dinner itself was a warm blur. Chance told a half-true story about hiking with Rose and getting lost. Kelli told Luke not to hover so much or she'd wrap *him* in bubble wrap for the next twenty-three weeks.

Fern found herself laughing so hard she nearly inhaled her water when Rose threatened to ban Pictionary if Chance tried to sneak in made-up words again.

"It's just not right," Rose complained. "I love your brogue, don't get me wrong, but when you deliberately toss in nonsense words and drawl them out, I lose all concentration."

"Rose hates losing," Fern pointed out to everyone in the room.

"Being happily distracted by a sexy drawl is still a win, isn't it?" Kelli asked, which set Chance grinning and Luke curling an arm around her possessively.

Luke cleared his throat then gave it a shot. "If it's an accent you be craving, missy, look no farther than your lawfully wedded man."

Fern covered her mouth to stop from snickering, and Rose turned away to hide her smile.

Chance, however, had no mercy. "What the feck was that? You sound like a pirate who swallowed a toad."

"Very sexy," Cody agreed before letting out a guffaw.

"Time to get into our teams!" Chance declared, patting Luke on the shoulder as the man grinned good-naturedly. Once the table was cleared and the coffee poured, Chance slapped a big sketch pad down in the center like a proud king revealing a treasure. "Kelli and Luke. Me and Rose. Cody, you're stuck with the tiny tyrant."

Fern threw her napkin at him. "I demand a recount."

"Sit down," Rose ordered, her grin wicked. "Before I switch you with Chance and *you'll* have to figure out my drawings all night."

Cody patted the empty chair next to him. "Might as well accept your fate, sweetheart."

"Better you than Rose. She once had to draw a house, and none of us got it right." Fern slid into the seat, pressing her knee firmly against his under the table. "Still, try not to embarrass me."

His reply was low enough that no one else heard. "Only plan on embarrassing you later. Not here."

Her cheeks went molten. She retaliated by grabbing the

marker and the first prompt, sketching so hard the tip of the pen squeaked before ripping the paper.

Chance cackled. "Solid start, Fern."

"Shut it!" she offered back, half mortified that she was so comfortable teasing the man who was, in fact, her boss.

Cody leaned close, his arm brushing hers as he squinted at her terrible drawing. She tried not to melt at the smell of him—warm skin, clean soap, a hint of the scent of the ranch that always clung to Red Boot's barns.

"I could have sworn you knew how to draw," he murmured. "Are you sandbagging it?"

She snickered. "I never cheat."

He leaned back, studied her frantic lines, and calmly said, "No, you're right. It's clearly an alien invasion."

"No freaking way," Chance howled. "Cheater!"

"Wait, I was right?" Shock tinged Cody's voice before his grin widened. "I mean, of course, I'm right. There's talent on both sides of this team."

"Horseshoes up his ass," Luke offered dryly.

They played until their sides hurt from laughing. Chance guessed "spaceship" for everything. Luke threatened to withhold foot rubs if Kelli didn't stop deliberately drawing what looked like cats with six legs.

Through it all, Fern let her shoulder lean heavier into Cody's, drinking in the way their secret felt safe here. Hidden in plain sight, surrounded by people they loved.

When Kelli finally called mercy and pushed away from the table to claim the best spot on the couch, Fern helped cap the markers and fold the paper for the recycle bin.

Cody caught her hand as she stacked the last sheet on top of the others.

"Let me," he murmured. His thumb swept over her knuckles, quick and gentle.

Her breath caught. He shouldn't do that here—

Chance's voice cut through her thoughts. "Hey, Cody. Walk Fern home, yeah? It's dark already, and while it's not Samhain yet, who knows what ghosts and ghoulies are about."

Cody winked over his shoulder. "Sure, bro."

Fern mock-glared at Chance but made no move to protest. She liked this. Being tucked into Cody's orbit with no one the wiser.

Instead of leading her across the yard, though, Cody took her to his truck. She didn't even pretend to sit prim. She scooted over on the bench seat until his thigh pressed warm and solid against hers. He slipped his arm around her shoulders, pulled her close.

"You're taking me straight home, right?" she teased, trying for stern. "All three blocks?"

Cody snorted, pressing a kiss to her temple. "Sure, sweetheart. Straight home."

EXCEPT HE DIDN'T.

Twenty minutes later, the truck bumped off the main road, tires crunching along the gravel loop behind Miller's old hayfield. Stars spilled across the clear black sky, big and reckless the way only prairie nights allowed.

He killed the engine. The sudden quiet pressed around them, broken only by the faint chorus of crickets and Fern's soft, eager breath.

"You lied," she said, accusing but with an enthusiasm that made his pulse trip.

"I'm a man of my word." He kept a straight face best he could. "I said *straight home.* Didn't say when or from where."

She swatted his shoulder, but he caught her wrist and tugged her closer. "Come here."

She went easily, slipping across the seat into his lap with a soft giggle that turned to a gasp when he slid a hand under her sweater.

"Cold?" he asked.

"Not even close," she shot back, threading the fingers of her right hand into his hair. Brushing the tips of the small fingers of her left limb over the soft threads as well.

It was different, but it was *her* different, so it was perfect.

He tipped his head to kiss her slow and thoroughly. Her lips tasted like apple crisp, the hint of a secret smile curling them at the corners. She made a quiet noise when he bit gently at her bottom lip, her hips shifting restlessly against his thigh.

"Truck bed?" she murmured against his mouth.

"Truck bed."

They tumbled into the brisk night, giggling like teenagers as he pulled an old wool blanket from behind the seat. She climbed up first, his hands steadying her hips as she crawled onto the open platform.

When he joined her, she was already half-settled on her back, hair a dark halo against the scratchy blanket, eyes bright even in the shadows.

"You," she said, tugging at his shirt buttons, "are overdressed."

"Bossy," he murmured, helping her with the last stubborn snap. Her hand was small yet sure, pushing fabric aside until she could skim her palm over his chest.

She hummed appreciatively, leaning up to press open-mouthed kisses over his collarbone. He growled low in his throat, rolling her gently under him. The stars above wheeled lazy and bright, distant witnesses to the way her fingers found the buckle of his belt.

"Slow down, greedy," he teased.

"Make me."

He pushed up, twisting to rest his back against the truck cab, hauling her into his lap until her knees bracketed his hips. She laughed into his mouth when he nipped her lip again, both of them breathless, drunk on each other.

He slid both hands under the hem of her sweater this time, thumbs tracing slow circles over the soft skin just beneath her bra line. She shivered and pressed closer, digging her fingers into his hair to tug his mouth back to hers.

God, she tasted like cinnamon and sinful secrets. He angled his head, deepened the kiss until it went from playful to desperate, all tongue and wet sighs. She scraped her hand down his chest, nails catching lightly, making him grunt against her lips.

"Careful," he murmured, the words coming out low and ragged. "I'm only human."

She rocked her hips over him deliberately, eyes dark and wicked. "I know exactly how human you are."

The friction made his vision blur. He caught her hips and forced them still for a second while he sucked a mark into the soft skin just below her jaw. She gasped, breath hitching into a soft laugh that dissolved into another moan when he bit gently and then soothed the spot with his tongue.

Fern tugged at the hem of her own sweater, half-yanking it up until he helped peel it off altogether. The night air made her skin pebble with goosebumps, but when he bent his head to plant kisses along her collarbone, she only arched closer, greedy for every inch of him.

He slipped the straps of her bra down, slower now, savouring the way her breath caught. His palms cupped the soft weight of her breasts, thumbs brushing over already-hard peaks before he lowered his head to taste her properly.

"Cody—" Her voice cracked on his name. She clutched his shoulders, fingers flexing when he drew one nipple into his mouth, rolling it gently with his tongue. Her hips rocked again, this time with no pretense of teasing.

"You're gonna break me, sweetheart," he murmured against her skin, the words vibrating into her chest.

"Promise?" she shot back, trembling slightly.

He laughed, low and dark, and shifted his mouth to her other breast, giving it the same attention until her soft gasps turned to tiny pleading sounds that nearly undid him completely.

He dragged one hand down her stomach, feeling the flutter of her belly under his touch as he popped the button of her jeans again, pushing inside to find her warm, slick, ready. He worked her with slow precision, matching every flick of his fingers with a filthy, adoring kiss to her throat or the tender curve beneath her ear.

"Look at you," he rasped, voice hoarse with pride and hunger. "So damn perfect. All mine."

Her hips bucked helplessly, and she buried her face in his neck, biting his shoulder to keep quiet. He hissed at the sharp sting, loving it, loving her.

She was trembling now, on the edge. He pressed his thumb harder, circled, and watched her fall apart right there in his lap under a sky wide enough to swallow every secret they'd ever kept.

When she came, she cried his name, a broken whisper lost to the wind. Her nails dug half-moons into his skin, and he wanted every mark.

He didn't stop kissing her. Not even when she sagged against him, her face buried in his throat.

After a minute, she drew back, cheeks flushed, lips kiss-swollen. She traced his mouth with a fingertip, then lower, down the stubble at his jaw, the line of his throat.

"I can—" she started, but he shook his head, catching her hand and pressing it flat over his heart.

"Not tonight." He kissed her palm, then her wrist, feeling her pulse race against his lips. "I'm so damn happy just like this. Trust me, sweetheart, next time, there's not gonna be a single inch of you I don't taste slowly."

She laughed softly, the sound sleepy and wicked at once. "You promise a lot of very good things."

He tugged her back down, rolling her gently until they lay tangled side by side on the old blanket in the truck bed. Above them, the stars wheeled on, silent witnesses.

Cody brushed her hair back from her temple, staring at her as if he could memorize her face by moonlight alone.

"Yeah," he whispered. "I promise."

Above them, the prairie sky spread on forever, full of stars, secrets, and the promise of every kiss yet to come.

6

———————

hanksgiving at the Fields house didn't look like the kind of big sit-down dinners Cody remembered from growing up with his mom's side of the family. Then it had been all starched napkins and forced conversation from people who saw each other so rarely they had nothing more in common than familial blood.

At Ivy and Walker's place, it was more like organized chaos. Laughter in every corner, little kids racing through legs, potluck-style dishes lined up across the island and kitchen counter as if they were an army waiting for the horn to blow *Charge*.

Cody loaded his plate, ducked past Fern who was deep in conspiratorial talk with her mom and Ivy, and found an empty spot beside Ashton Stewart. The semi-retired foreman from Silver Stone ranch had become *Grandpa* to the Fields family by marriage, but the man wore the title as easy as an old pair of boots.

Across the table, Harper Fields, seven going on

unstoppable, peppered Ashton with questions between bites of pumpkin pie.

"Do chickens all lay eggs?"

Ashton looked down at her seriously. "If they know what's good for them, they do."

"Can horses swim?"

"Only if you pay 'em enough," Ashton deadpanned then winked at Cody.

"Don't believe everything he tells you, sweetheart," Cody warned before leaning forward to add, "Some horses don't even wait to put on their swimsuits and rush right into the water wearing only their birthday suits."

Ashton chuckled, eyes twinkling. He leaned back, one arm draped over Harper's chair. "Good man here, Miss Harper. Knows which end of a horse to pat and when to keep his mouth shut. Better foreman than I ever was."

"Lies and slander," Cody said, but pride warmed him through.

He caught Fern's gaze across the room. A quick smile flashed between them in the middle of the tightly controlled family storm.

Yeah, he liked this. Liked being woven into the edges of their messy, warm tangle.

Liked even more knowing he'd sneak Fern away later when nobody was watching and kiss her silly for a good long while.

By Wednesday, the easy warmth of pie and too many extra helpings gave way to work that wouldn't end. Cody's phone buzzed just as he dropped into the office chair to deal with a fresh list of supply orders.

> Fern: I have a second to breathe. So, hi. You still kicking?

Cody: Kicking, running, riding, hurrying. Who ordered this delivery of chaos?

Fern: You too? I swear I'm constantly shoving square pegs into round holes. But I'm having fun. Mostly. Did you know that it's possible to upload a file big enough to stall out the gaming matrix of the Painting with The Masters program?

Cody: I did not know that. You'll figure it out. You and those computers are besties.

Fern: It's still a pain in the butt.

Cody: Just think how good it will feel to fix the problem and save my brother's hide again.

Fern: He'll be grateful. I'll have to tell him I did it though, because he never even tries to use the computers anymore. Not for anything, unless he can't help it. I'm afraid I'm enabling a Luddite tech-hating monster.

Cody: On a different topic, want to get together soon?

The three dots danced. Then disappeared. Appeared again.

His gut clenched. Ridiculous how one text bubble could knot him up tighter than barbed wire. And the idea that she might not want to see him?

A blare of sound suddenly chirped from his phone. He answered so fast he heard her giggle.

"Attachment failure," Fern admitted between laughs. "I zigged when I should have zagged, and my hook jammed and knocked my phone to the floor. Again. I can't type on a phone that's not in my hand."

"Your bionic arm needs a tune-up, sweetheart." He shifted,

propping his boots on the box beside the desk. "Want to swap hands?"

"Ha-ha. You're not allowed to be sweeter than me. Stop it and tell me more about our next date."

A grin spread across his face despite the long day. "Friday. You. Me. A bunch of goofy tasks at Red Boot. Call your crew. I'm short a few warm bodies to test this corporate bonding circus the oil company's renting the ranch for."

Fern's suspicious hum echoed loudly in his ear. "Goofy sounds fine, but aren't those things usually full of physical challenges like heaving yourself over too-tall walls? Because I don't heave. With or without my spare parts."

"No climbing walls or dangling off bridges. Worst thing is probably trying to herd balloons into a pen with pool noodles. It'll be good for a laugh."

She snorted. "Deal. I can already assure you that Charity and Dustin will be in because they're in town and were just going to Rough Cut. I could ask Shim."

Cody's teeth clicked together. "Shim. Right. *Fine.* I'm feeling generous. Bring him. Better yet, tell him to bring a friend."

She cackled. "You're not jealous of Shim, are you?"

"Of course not," he lied.

"He's only a friend," she assured him.

"Good."

Which made her laugh as she hung up.

A couple days later, the autumn air sliced around them, crisp and bright, rustling the last stubborn leaves still clinging to the big poplars by Red Boot's main arena.

Cody stood beside Zach, arms folded, as the crew lined up like misfit recruits: Fern, Charity, Dustin, Shim and, tucked half behind Shim's shoulder, a new face.

Dark hair, warm brown eyes that flicked up at Cody then darted away.

Cody cocked a brow and gentled his tone. "This your plus-one, Shim?"

Shim cleared his throat. If ears could glow, his were practically neon. "Uh, yeah. This is Amanda. She's new at Silver Stone. Figured she'd come along so she could take a look around here and then appreciate what a *proper* ranch looks like when we get home."

Cody barked a laugh. It was going to be like that, was it? "Careful, or I'll have Zach poach her before you make it back through the gate."

Amanda's cheeks flushed pink, but her shy smile remained. Fern winked at her behind Shim's back.

"All right, pirates," Zach boomed, shaking out a ridiculous parchment roll as if he'd unearthed it in a treasure chest. "Gather up for your official corporate-morale chaos. I didn't make these up, but I *did* promise to document every disaster for the oil company's HR department."

He flicked the scroll open, nearly backhanding Cody on the nose, and rattled off the teams. "Okay, so we've got Dustin with Fern, Charity with Shim, and—"

Before he could continue, Dustin raised both hands. "Whoa, no, no. I want Charity. No offense, Fern, but she's the only one who won't drop me on my ass."

Fern fake gasped. "Wow, Dustin. Betrayal, like a dagger right to the heart."

Charity just preened. "Smart man."

Zach rolled his eyes. "Fine. Dustin and Charity. Shim and Amanda—you're welcome. Which leaves you—" he pointed at Cody and Fern "—to babysit each other. Try not to break anything that costs money, okay?"

Cody shot Fern a sidelong grin. "Guess you're stuck with me, sweetheart."

Her answering smile cranked up the heat in his chest like a sunbeam. "Oh, the hardship."

Zach brandished the scroll like a royal decree. "Task One: Ping Pong Panic. Rules are simple. Each pair bounces the ball back and forth as long as you can. Max time is two minutes. If more than one team hits two minutes total, we break the tie by going again and counting total bounces. Got it?"

What he got was a chorus of good-natured groans.

Still, Fern raised her paddle like a rapier. "Got it. We're about to win."

Dustin pointed at her dramatically. "You drop everything. I don't trust you."

Fern stuck her tongue out. "This is why you're not my partner, traitor."

Amanda snickered at Shim's side. Shim puffed up like a rooster. Cody bit back another laugh.

"On my whistle." Zach yelled. "*Go.*"

Paddles flashed. Balls bounced.

Twice— Three times—

They didn't even have time to develop a rhythm before disaster struck.

Fern hit the ball a little too hard then squealed when Cody's overzealous save deflected their ball straight into the back of Dustin's head. Dustin flailed, his paddle swinging, and Charity shrieked. The errant shot sent their ball ricocheting off Shim's thigh. Amanda, halfway through a giggle fit, fumbled so hard her paddle smacked her own knee.

Only Shim and Amanda managed a half-decent run, mostly because Shim hovered so close he body-blocked every stray bounce.

Zach wheezed with laughter, clipboard shaking. "Okay, corporate is screwed. Next up is Balloon Herding. You have two minutes to corral as many balloons into your pen as you can, using only pool noodles. No hands, no cheating, no mercy. Ready?"

Cody leaned down, voice low at Fern's ear as they shuffled to where an enormous mound of brightly coloured balloons waited at the start line. "We're doomed, aren't we?"

She bumped his hip with hers, eyes sparkling. "Never say die."

~

ZACH'S WHISTLE split the air, and suddenly everyone was swinging foam noodles at rogue balloons like underpaid circus clowns.

Fern lunged for a pink balloon that bobbed just out of reach. Cody dove after another, narrowly missing her by inches before skidding sideways on the dusty arena floor.

"Too slow, cowboy!" she taunted, batting a purple balloon straight into their pen.

He spun around and bonked his noodle lightly against her rear. "Don't sass your teammate."

She stuck her tongue out only to yelp when a blue balloon bounced off her forehead. Cody's noodle whapped it back into play with ninja precision.

Nearby, Dustin was yelling instructions at Charity. "No, left! No, *your* left—"

Charity whirled and pinged him square in the ribs with her noodle. "I know my left, you walking disaster!"

Shim and Amanda were the only calm ones. She giggled every time Shim barked, "Stay on target, we almost got 'em!" as if they were defusing bombs instead of wrangling dollar store balloons.

By the time Zach called time, Fern was breathless and doubled over laughing.

"Count 'em up!" Zach ordered. "Team Dustin-Charity: nine balloons. Shim-Amanda: thirteen! Cody-Fern..." He squinted into the pen. "That's more than I expected. Twelve. Not terrible."

Cody slung an arm around Fern's shoulders as she leaned into his side, both still panting.

She grinned up at him. "Nice wrangling there, cowboy."

Zach waved them toward the far side of the arena. "Next up, Beam Walk. Which is just fancy talk for 'don't fall off this two by four while balancing a cup of water.'"

Dustin groaned dramatically. "We get to break ankles *and* look like idiots? Perfect."

Zach raised a brow. "It's all of four inches off the ground. I think your ankles are safe."

Fern gave Cody a sly glance. "I used to pretend I was a tightrope walker on our porch railing as a kid. Piece of cake."

"Sweetheart, if you eat dirt, I'm not catching you."

She waggled her brows. "You *better*."

Turns out, balancing water while giggling at your secret boyfriend is not a recipe for success.

Fern was halfway across the wobbly beam, cup bobbing precariously, when Cody, following close behind her, muttered, "Don't wiggle that cute ass at me, or I'll drop mine too."

She snorted so hard she choked. Her foot slipped, arms pinwheeling, and Cody lunged forward with a swear, catching her waist just before she toppled sideways.

The water hit his shoulder, soaking his flannel.

She shrieked with laughter as they both tumbled off the beam, landing in a heap on the soft sawdust.

Over their heads, Zach bellowed, "Disqualified! But bonus points for entertainment value!"

Fern twisted under Cody's arms, curly hair full of wood shavings, laughing so hard her ribs hurt. She wriggled free just as Shim jogged over to help haul her upright.

"Smooth, Fields," Shim teased, flicking a piece of straw out of her curls. "Graceful as ever."

"Hey, I stuck the landing...with help," she shot back, bumping her hip against Cody's leg with mock innocence.

Cody smothered a grin, dusting hay off his shirt. "Next time I'm wearing body armor."

They plowed through the last event. A ridiculous blindfold-and-guide relay where each pair had to direct one partner through a maze of hay bales using only shouted instructions.

Fern and Cody tanked that one too, mostly because she was snickering so hard she kept confusing his directions until he declared, "I'm trading you for Amanda next time!"

She gasped dramatically. "Rude!"

He stole a quick kiss under cover of the hay maze wall. "You're still my favourite cowgirl."

Zach called it. "All right, corporate event crash test dummies, you did Red Boot proud—or at least hilariously average. I'm giving everyone a free beer and calling it a win."

Cheers and exhausted high fives flew around. Dustin bear-hugged Charity until she squealed. Shim gave Amanda a quick, bashful shoulder squeeze that made her blush bright enough to rival the sunset.

Cody threw a playful arm around Amanda's shoulders too. "Anytime you want to moonlight at a real ranch, you're welcome at Red Boot, Amanda."

Shim snapped his head up, scowling. "Hey—!"

Fern swatted Cody's bicep as she stepped into his hug. Her voice was a mock-growl only he could hear. "Watch it, buster."

Cody bent to murmur at her temple, grinning like a devil. "Just getting Shim's goat. You're the only cowgirl for me."

Her chest did that fluttery flip it always did when he dropped his voice like that. She squeezed him back hard, and for a second, it didn't matter who was watching.

Sometimes secrets were worth keeping, if only because they made moments like this—goofy, breathless, *theirs*—shine ten times brighter.

7

____

Petra's November birthday party was a cheerful riot of chaos. Fairy lights were strung across the beams of the artists' studio at High Water ranch, music spilling through open doors, with clusters of people laughing around paper plates piled high with cake and snacks.

Fern drifted between her best friend Charity, who kept stealing bites off Dustin's plate, and a knot of her sisters' friends near the makeshift dance floor. But her attention kept wandering. Across the room, near the corner by a tiny buffet table with spiked cider, Cody stood half in shadow.

He wasn't looking at her—not directly. He chatted with Chance and Luke Stone, nodded at something Petra squealed about as she danced past. But every few minutes his eyes found hers, and the force of that quiet heat sent Fern's stomach swooping in the most delicious way.

They were good at this now. The pretending. Smothering private laughter with polite small talk, brushing too close in a crowded space and shrugging it off with an easy grin. But tonight, Fern couldn't hold it in anymore. Not when he kept tipping his beer back with that lazy smirk and half-winking as if he knew exactly what she'd do if she could get him alone for ten minutes.

It would have been fun to be more explicit in the text message she'd sent him when he'd walked in the door, but she kept from spilling the beans about what she'd arranged.

Cody was fire to her soul, but he'd remained far too controlled for her liking. It was time to take matters into her own hands.

Charity elbowed her gently. "You're staring. Spill it. What's he done now?"

"Nothing," Fern hissed, cheeks warming at the idea her friends might guess the direction of her thoughts. "It's nothing."

Dustin snorted behind his cider mug. "It's never nothing with you two. He rope you into some wild activity again?"

Fern rolled her eyes. "Maybe."

Before she could defend herself further, a warm hand curled around her elbow.

"Excuse me, folks," Cody said, voice all easy charm. "Mind if I steal my partner? She owes me a rematch."

Charity snickered. "Playing solo Ping Pong Panic again? You two are worse than kids."

"Have fun losing, Cody," Dustin added with a smirk.

Fern squeaked as Cody tugged her away, weaving past the buffet table and the cluster of gossipy aunts lingering by the pies. She elbowed him lightly. "A rematch? Really?"

"I panicked." His grin was a white flash. "You said something about a view you wanted to show me?"

"Welcome to your private tour of High Water ranch," Fern said.

They slipped out the side door, their boots crunching over the snow. Fern shivered, tugging her coat tighter, and Cody immediately slipped out of his own to drape it over her shoulders without breaking stride.

She guided him toward the old animal rescue barn at the far edge of the property. The structure remained exactly as Fern remembered from the years of her grandmother running the shelter, with faded red siding, a big loft door, and the smell of straw and old timber. When the family had visited, Fern used to slip away and hide in the loft, curled up in a makeshift haybale chair to read, or to stare over the fields to the mountains rising in the west.

Inside, it was quieter, though the faint strains of music drifted through the rafters from the neighbouring building where the party continued. Cody followed her up the loft ladder, then she casually paused to slip the wooden latch that would lock the trapdoor.

She didn't want any other privacy seekers interrupting them tonight.

"Thank you for the coat, gallant knight," she teased, shrugging out of it and spreading it over a hay bale near the big shuttered windows. She pushed them open, letting moonlight spill across the wooden floor.

"Best I could manage on short notice," he shot back, but his eyes were soft as he settled beside her. He pulled her in, tucking her into his side, letting her burrow her cold fingers under the hem of his shirt without a flinch.

They sat like that for a while, the music a faint heartbeat beyond them, their breath puffing little clouds in the chilly air as they stared into a star-filled sky. Outside the artists' studio to their left, someone lit a bonfire, and the scent of woodsmoke carried on the crisp winter night air.

Fern traced random patterns on Cody's chest, feeling him shiver every time she dipped her fingers lower.

"Tell me something about little Fern," he murmured. "Something you don't share at family dinners."

She laughed into his coat collar then sobered. "Okay. You remember I was adopted as a newborn, right?"

He nodded, rubbing his chin over the top of her head.

"Well, people always want to ask, but they chicken out. So no, I wasn't put up for adoption because of my arm. My birth mom had already arranged it all with Sophie and Malachi. She wanted me to have them from day one. The arm was just fate being weird. It was never really a big deal."

"Still hard though, I bet," Cody said softly, nose brushing her temple. "People suck sometimes."

"They do." Fern tipped her head and caught his lips in a slow, lingering kiss that chased the chill away. "But it's not the missing hand that's hard. Like, tonight I'm not even wearing my prothesis, and it's fine. It's the constant fight to exist how I am. No explanations, no edits to make strangers comfortable. Just Fern. Every day, every minute. Some days I wish I could wake up, do the right thing, and never feel as if it's a battle."

"I think you do it brilliantly," he murmured, his mouth sliding along her jaw. "You wake up and you're *you*. And you're... Christ, you're perfect, you know that?"

She snorted, pressing her forehead to his. "Flatterer. Now it's your turn. Tell me a terrible teenage Cody story."

"All right," Cody said, a smile already tugging at his lips. "When I was thirteen, Chance was eighteen, and he'd just gotten his first real car. He told Mom and Dad he was heading out for a late movie at a classic drive-in with the guys, so I figured, perfect. I'll sneak in the back and tag along. Didn't want to ask 'cause I knew he'd say no. So I hid under an old blanket and waited him out like a little stalker."

Fern was already snickering. "You did not."

"Swear to God. I thought we were going to hit a drive-in,

eat popcorn, maybe even hit a second show. Turned out his 'guys' were just him and a girl he'd been dying to impress. They pull up to the drive-in lot, I pop out all triumphant. Surprise! Third wheel right here!"

She laughed so hard she snorted, burying her face in his neck.

"Poor Chance," Cody chuckled, nuzzling her hair. "He paid for my ticket, bought me a bucket of popcorn bigger than my head, and then had to watch Spider-Man with his little brother perched right behind him while his date glared knives at me for the rest of the night. He didn't talk to me for a week."

She doubled over laughing, half muffled against his shirt. "You little menace."

"Only for him. Always for him." Cody sighed contentedly, brushing her hair back. "We both got good families, huh?"

"The best." She stretched up and kissed him again, deeper this time. Beneath them, a few new voices drifted near the bonfire outside, but Cody's hand curved over her hip, grounding her.

It was time.

"Got something to show you," she murmured, tugging him back into the shadows of the loft. There, tucked between hay bales, she'd spread a thick quilt and stashed two lantern-style flashlights.

"Fern?" There was a question in his eyes along with heat.

"I helped my sister set up food for the party and took advantage of the time to slip up here," she whispered. "I want you."

She'd thought he might hesitate, but he didn't. Her breath caught as he guided her onto the blankets, covering her with his warmth.

"It's cold," she warned, even as she tugged at his shirt hem.

"I'll keep you warm."

She laughed, soft and wild. When he kissed her this time, she let the November chill be chased away, bit by heated bit.

SHE LAUGHED INTO HIS MOUTH, soft and wicked, and the sound vibrated down every nerve in his body like a spark struck too close to dry grass.

Cody kissed her deeper, muffling her amusement, his hands already under her sweater, skating warm palms over bare skin that felt like satin gone molten under his fingertips. Outside, muffled music and laughter from the bonfire drifted up, but inside the hayloft, it was just them and the hush of winter wind.

He'd been content being patient, but he was glad the wait was over.

He tugged her sweater higher, groaning when she wriggled to help, and then her bra too, simple, soft cotton and lace, and her breath caught when the cool air licked over her flushed skin.

"God, look at you," he rasped, brushing his thumbs over her tight peaks. Fern arched her back, pushing into his palms, and the sound she made nearly snapped every thread of restraint left in him.

She tugged at his shirt in retaliation, nails scraping across his ribs as she shoved the fabric up and off. They broke the kiss long enough to untangle sleeves and dump it on the quilt, then he was on her again, pinning her forearms above her head for a heartbeat just to watch her eyes flare wide with heat.

"Bossy," she whispered.

"You like me bossy," he shot back, dipping his mouth to her

throat, then lower, dragging his tongue across the soft swell of her breast.

Fern gasped, her legs shifting restlessly under him, thighs brushing his hips in silent invitation.

"Say it," he murmured, teeth grazing her nipple. "Tell me."

"I like you bossy," she panted, hips tilting up as if she could pull him deeper already. "Cody— God, *please—*"

He chuckled low in his chest and shifted down her body, mouthing his way across her ribs, her belly. His fingers worked her jeans open, the button popping free so easily that she made a small, embarrassed huff.

"Problem?" he teased, brushing his knuckles along the waistband of her panties.

"You're too good at that."

He bit lightly at her hip bone in reply, then tugged jeans and panties off in one slow drag down her legs. The cold nipped at bare skin, but his mouth followed the trail, pressing hot kisses behind his hands until she was squirming and whispering, *"Please, please, please."*

He settled back on his knees for a second, just to take her in. Hair dark against the old quilt, chest heaving, every inch of her soft and flushed and so damn *his* that it made his chest ache.

Fern reached for him, dragging him down until his mouth covered hers again, greedy and hot. She tasted sweet, her fingers fisting in his hair when he rocked his hips forward, the hard line of his cock nudging where she was already wet and ready.

She hissed at the contact, nails scraping his scalp. "Cody, oh—"

"Shh, baby. I got you." He slipped a hand between them, sliding his fingers over her slick heat, teasing her clit with soft circles until her legs trembled around him.

Every sweet gasp made him harder. He pushed two fingers inside her, slow and deep, watching her eyes flutter shut as her lips parted in a silent plea.

"Good?" he asked, voice like gravel now.

"Better than good," she gasped, clutching at his biceps, her short left arm braced at his shoulder as she rocked her hips to meet each thrust of his fingers. "Don't stop, don't stop—"

He didn't. He ground the heel of his palm against her clit, pressing kisses into her throat as she came apart under him, soft cries muffled against his bare shoulder.

When her shudders eased, she dragged him down for another kiss, tasting him slow and deep until he was half-crazed with the need to be inside her.

Fern rolled her hips up into his, playful and daring. "Switch."

"Switch?" he echoed, half-laughing even as she shoved at his chest.

She pushed until he gave in, flopping onto his back with a muffled grunt. She scrambled to straddle him, knees bracing in the hay on either side of his hips.

Fern fumbled for something beside the flashlight lantern.

"You ready?" she whispered as she held a condom in the air.

"Yes. But you're not touching me or we'll be done before we start," he warned. He shoved down his jeans and underwear then snatched the condom from her and rolled it on with frantic speed.

The glow from the lantern caught the curve of her breasts as she sank down onto him in one smooth, wicked motion.

"Jesus— *Fern*—" He grabbed her hips, fighting the urge to buck upward. She felt too good, too hot and tight and wet around him, and her satisfied expression turned even more smug at his helpless groan.

"Payback," she teased, leaning forward to kiss him as she rolled her hips, slow and sinuous, a rhythm that had him biting back curses.

"Gonna be the death of me," he groaned.

Her laugh was pure mischief. She braced her hand on his chest and rode him slow, teasing at first, then faster as the tension coiled tight in both of them.

Somewhere beneath the hayloft, the first *pop* of fireworks split the air, startling a yelp from Fern that turned into helpless moans as coloured sparks danced against the loft window.

"You planned fireworks?" he gasped.

Fern moved over him with that perfect drag that made his eyes roll back. "I wanted you to see stars."

He gripped her hips tighter. "Don't stop, sweetheart, I swear—"

The barn lit in flickers of red and gold and blue, loud pops echoing outside while they moved together in the shadows, tangled up in heat and secrets and muffled laughter they couldn't hold back.

She bent low, pressing her forehead to his, breath breaking against his lips. "Cody—oh, *God*—"

He surged up, kissing her hard as the last tight coil in his gut snapped. Fireworks exploded in time with the shudder that ripped through him when she fell apart again, this time around him.

For a heartbeat, he swore he saw stars both inside and out.

Fern slumped over him, snickering against his sweaty chest as another distant boom rattled the old barn walls. Cody pressed a sloppy kiss to her temple, still trying to catch his breath.

"Fireworks and you. Overachiever," he teased.

"I knew Tansy planned them. The timing was all destiny."

Cody laughed so hard his ribs hurt.

Eventually, the cold found them again, nipping at damp skin and flushed cheeks. Between kisses that kept them tangled longer than necessary, they fumbled back into their clothes. Inside-out underwear, socks half lost under hay bales, her bra a twisted casualty until he helped hook it properly, their amusement a warm hug around them.

Fern tugged her sweater into place and gave him a mock glare when he caught her waist for one more lingering kiss. "We look guilty as sin."

"We *are* guilty as sin," Cody shot back, holding her close enough to bite her lower lip playfully.

She swatted his chest and ducked under his arm, flicking off the faux lanterns as they snuck back down the ladder. Outside, the party goers were returning to the bonfire, people bundled in jackets and cradling mugs of something hot now that the fireworks were done.

Fern drifted toward Charity and Dustin, cheeks glowing, eyes full of secrets only Cody would ever know.

He let himself remain near the barn's darker edge, wholehearted happiness lingering as he watched her melt back into her friends, perfectly casual.

Nobody suspected a thing.

Later, back at Red Boot, the high still hummed under his skin as he walked through the main barn, trailing his hand along warm horse flanks.

He clipped a lead to Lonesome Charlie's halter, murmuring praise.

Cody's left hand opened—just...*opened*—without permission. The rope slipped free, flopping useless in the hay.

He flexed his fingers, frowning when they obeyed this time, perfectly normal, but with a sticky, slow-motion sensation that lingered like a ghost in his bones.

All the sweet joy of the day wiped aside. High to low. Heaven to dread. All in a heartbeat.

He swallowed hard, eyes drifting skyward through the barn rafters, whispering to no one, *"What the hell is going on?"*

8

---

ody had never thought the phrase *too good to be true* would fit his ordinary ranch life. Yet here he was. Daily chores and worthwhile activities mixed with catching Fern's laughter like sunshine, stealing kisses when no one was watching.

No one blinked at the time they spent together. Not Tansy, not Ivy, not Fern's parents. They all thought he and Fern were just friends.

Maybe they *did* have the word tattooed on their foreheads.

Some days he almost believed it himself. If he didn't look too closely. If he didn't notice how everything took an extra heartbeat now when it came to spending time together.

This early December morning the ranch was hushed under fresh snow, pale sunlight slanting through frost-tipped trees behind the arena. He paused in the feed shed, breath misting in the quiet, and stared at his left hand as the grain scoop he held jittered uncontrollably.

Cody shook out his wrist, glaring as if that would bully it back to normal.

It calmed. His mind didn't.

Not even an hour later, out by the corral fence, he waved to a couple headed out on a trail ride, and his left shoulder locked up like a rusted hinge. He managed a smile for the paying customers, but his brain shrieked in fear.

Back in his cabin that night, he sat post-shower on the edge of his bed. His clean flannel shirt was nearly buttoned, but he'd fumbled the last button three times before giving up.

Cold wind rattled the window behind him, snow hissing across the sill.

What. The. Hell.

His phone buzzed on the mattress beside his knee. Fern's name bloomed on the screen like a promise.

Fern: You. Me. Leftover pie and a sappy Christmas movie. Tonight.

He should have leapt for that. But his hand jerked when he reached for the phone, the tremor flaring as if mocking him.

He typed carefully, cursing inside as he awkwardly used one hand.

Cody: Rain check. Long day. Early night.

He hit Send and hated himself.

She sent back a pouty emoji and three heart stickers. He almost broke and said *Screw it, come over,* but he couldn't. Not until he knew what the fuck was happening to him.

That night, as the barn lights glowed faint behind the living room window, Cody sat hunched over his laptop, the hum of the cabin heater filling the silence.

He typed *hand tremor* into the search bar. Then *hand tremors in men under forty.* Then *loss of fine motor control.*

Maybe it was stupid, going online, but he didn't know what else to do. This first, surely.

The hits he got back were quick and clear. Mayo Clinic. Parkinson's Foundation. Patient forums where strangers poured out stories that tangled in his gut.

The tremor started on one side. Slowness of movement. Progressive.

No cure.

Cody scrubbed a palm over his face, catching his reflection in the dark window. He looked older than he should. Tired. A tightness lingered in his neck now too. An ache that wouldn't quit even when he rotated his shoulders.

The page blurred. He didn't realize his thumb was jumping again until he reached for the mouse and knocked it to the floor. It skittered under the bunk like a small, cowardly thing.

"It's probably nothing," he told the flickering cursor.

The cursor blinked back, patient, yet unbelieving.

The next morning, he was on the phone with Dr. Sydney Jeremiah's clinic. It took a couple days before he got a phone appointment, reciting symptoms to her in a voice that felt wrong. Far too confident, far too level. "I'd appreciate you not mentioning this to anyone yet," he added.

"Of course not. *Your body, your choice* applies to everyone." Dr. Jeremiah listened. Calm, kind. Promised she'd get him a consult as soon as she could, but it probably wouldn't be until the New Year. "Try to keep your stress levels low, Cody. We'll figure it out."

"Sure," he rasped, staring out the barn office window at the pale sun clawing through snow-covered pine branches. A cold wind rattled the siding. Horses moved like shadows at the far fence, steam rising from their backs.

He didn't say anything to Fern because... What was he supposed to say? *I seem to be falling apart at the seams.*

He dodged her texts for a few days with excuses. Fence checks, extra work with bookings at the ranch, needing extra rest. Every lie left him emptier than the last. He couldn't bear to open his yap and talk to her, though.

Talking made it feel real.

He didn't want real.

But not talking to Fern took far too much energy. Not being with her felt as if he had a limb missing, and the irony of that thought didn't escape him.

Which was why two days later, he scrolled flight options with numb fingers while the wind howled outside the cabin door.

When he found what he was looking for, he booked it fast: *Dublin. December 20th. Return date flexible.* The cursor pulsed like a heartbeat he couldn't slow down.

He told Zach, Karen, and Finn because the people paying his salary absolutely needed to know he was running off with barely a moment's notice.

Cody still didn't tell Fern. Not yet.

Chance caught him wrench-deep in the baler behind the arena on a brittle Tuesday morning. Snow squeaked under Chance's boots as he leaned into the open bay.

"You lost your mind, wee brother?"

Cody grunted, not looking up. "What do you want, Chance?"

Chance crossed his arms, expression sharp as the cold. "Not that he was telling tales out of term, but it came up in passing. Now I've heard and now I know. Zach says you're bailing to Ireland for Christmas. Family reunion I'm not invited to? Or something you're not saying?"

Changing position, Cody swore as his shoulder muscles froze. The bolt he'd loosened slid from his fingers and clinked off the frame.

His left hand just couldn't hold it.

"Just wanted to see my mom," he lied. "And Dad, of course."

Chance eyed him. That seeing-right-through-you look only an older brother could perfect. "You sure it's not about Fern?"

Cody scraped grease off his palms with a rag. "Leave it, Chance."

"You're not denying she means something to you."

"Drop it," Cody ordered with a hint of desperation.

A quiet settled, broken only by the horse paddock gate clanging somewhere behind them.

Finally, Chance's voice softened, the Irish burr thick. "You're an eejit. Some messes are worth sticking around to fix."

Cody turned away, pretending to hunt for a wrench. Pretending his whole chest hadn't squeezed at hearing that single truth.

Long after his brother left, Cody sat on the bench by the arena. The cold wind bit through his warmest jacket. He forced his left hand flat on his thigh yet watched as a faint tremor danced through the fingers.

He wanted Fern. He wanted her so bad his teeth ached with it. But wanting and deserving weren't the same thing.

Cody shut his eyes and pictured Fern's smile. The one that made him hope for forever.

Worth the mess, Chance said. Cody wasn't so sure *he* was.

She's worth everything, he thought. So he'd care enough to let her go if that's what it took to keep her whole.

THE SNICK of Fern's Bluetooth stylus whispered through the gallery's upper rooms. Below, Chance's voice drifted up now and then as he led a small school group past the new landscape series. Outside, Heart Falls slogged through an unexpected mid-December drizzle. Neither snow nor rain, just enough slush to smear the windows and grey the sky.

Fern forced herself to focus on the layout proofs for the spring art auction pamphlet. She highlighted an entire paragraph, deleted it, rewrote it, deleted it again.

Cody hadn't texted in three days.

Not since she'd sent him a dumb selfie. Her wrapped in a scarf with frost on her eyelashes, teasing him to come rescue her from freezing in the parking lot. Normally he'd fire back some smart remark. Instead...

Nothing.

Downstairs, the front door chimed and soft laughter mixed with the hush of December wind. A few minutes later, Chance's shoes thudded up the stairs.

He ducked under a hanging display of dried paper lanterns and propped himself against her desk. His expression was soft but edged in that big-brother caution Fern had learned to spot.

"Got a sec, sunshine?"

"Always." She twisted her stylus between her fingers, heart picking up speed. "What's up? If it's about the promo—"

"It's not gallery stuff."

Chance dragged a stool over, flipped it backward, and straddled it, arms folded over the backrest. He looked every inch a scruffy Irish artist. Paint under his fingernails, hair barely tamed by a halfhearted tie at his nape.

He didn't look like a hammer blow, but that's what his next words felt like .

"Cody's gone home for Christmas."

Fern stared. "Home— you mean Red Boot? Or Toronto—"

Chance's eyes softened. "Ireland."

The stylus slipped from her fingers, clattering on her tablet. "What? When?"

"He flew out this morning."

A rush of confusion and something cold crawled up her neck. "Why didn't he say— I mean, he didn't—"

"He didn't tell you," Chance finished gently. "Aye. I told him he was a feckin' eejit for it. For the record."

She opened her mouth. Closed it again.

"For how long?" she asked, her voice smaller than she liked.

Chance shrugged one shoulder. "Didn't say. Maybe a couple weeks. Maybe more."

For a moment, the bright lights of the loft seemed to flicker. A pulse behind her eyes she blamed on the gallery lighting. She blinked until the room sharpened again.

"I thought—" She bit the inside of her cheek. *You thought what, Fern? That he was too happy to leave you?* She'd made a wrong assumption at some point.

Chance must have read every word of her silence. He reached across the desk, brushing his knuckles against hers.

"I've known for a while, you know."

Her breath hitched. "Known what?"

"That you two are daft about each other." His grin creased the corners of his eyes. "It's not exactly subtle, little sister. Well, not to me, anyway."

Fern laughed, except it cracked in the middle and turned into something watery. "Does Rose know? About us being daft?"

"No. Which surprises me because she's usually more aware of things of the heart." Chance gave Fern's hand a gentle squeeze. "Your reasons to stay quiet are your reasons. Same for him. But I told him not to run. To fix whatever is wrong instead of hiding like a stubborn mule."

She swallowed, her throat gone tight enough to hurt. "Why didn't he say goodbye?"

Chance hesitated.

In that small moment of uncertainty, Fern had plenty of time to mentally list all the reasons Cody probably hadn't willingly put words to. Pride. Fear.

That quiet, heavy need he had to carry the weight alone.

"Don't exactly know, but he's a good man," Chance said softly. "Too good sometimes. Since you're not acting as if you two had a row, it's got to be something else. I'm pretty sure he loves you enough he thinks leaving is somehow protecting you."

Love. There was a word they hadn't even started to toss around, and yet...

She let the idea sink in, while outside, sleet hissed against the windows.

When she finally looked back at Chance, her voice was calm, but her heart banged around her ribs as if it wanted to leap straight across the ocean after his brother.

"I don't need protecting," she said.

Chance's smile curved lopsided. "Aye. Tell him that when you see him again."

Fern pushed to her feet and squared her shoulders. Her reflection in the glass beside the hallway looked the same as always. Black curls, warm eyes, arms hanging loose against her sides, no hiding or apology in her stance.

Same person she was a few hours ago. Except she was getting damn tired of waiting for the universe to get its shit together.

She bent to hug Chance, squeezing until he grunted.

"Thank you for telling me," she whispered into his flannel shirt.

"Thanks for making my brother smile more than I've ever seen," he murmured back. "At least until he lost his fecking head."

She stepped away, grabbed her bag from under the desk,

and made it halfway to the stairs before Chance's voice floated after her.

"You gonna chase him?"

Fern paused, hand on the railing, a spark of determination flickering to life in the hollow Cody's absence left behind. But he'd chosen this, so she'd honour that. At least for now.

"No," she called back. "But when he comes home, he'd better be ready."

9

———

The house was half-asleep in that lazy holiday stretch between Christmas and the New Year. Snow muffled the world beyond the windows; somewhere deep inside, the woodstove cracked and sighed.

Fern found her dad exactly where she knew he'd be. Sprawled on the big old sofa, sock feet crossed on the coffee table, half snoozing, half reading a battered Louis L'Amour novel.

She hovered in the doorway, arms crossed tight over her chest.

She'd had time to think more about Cody. And Cody's choices. To ponder the whys of his leaving and to really consider if she was ready and willing to sign up for more.

Answers hovered, but before locking them down, she needed to get some affirmation from the best man she knew.

Malachi didn't look up right away. He turned a page with deliberate calm then slid a glance over the top of his glasses. "Something on your mind, baby girl?"

She crossed the room before she could talk herself out of it,

84

dropped onto the rug at his feet, and leaned her shoulder against his knee.

She felt more than heard him close the book.

"I think," Fern murmured, staring into the fire's orange glow, "I've gotten involved with a man who doesn't know how to share what he's feeling. And he thinks not talking is the kindest thing he can do for me."

Silence. Only the crackle of burning logs and the old grandfather clock ticking steady in the hall.

Her dad's big hand settled on her crown, fingers petting her curls the same way he had when she was six and scraped her knee. As when she was fourteen and pissed off at rude comments about her arm.

Or when she was seventeen and swore she'd never need anyone in her life to feel complete.

"You cry over him every day?" Malachi asked finally.

Fern sniffed. "Not every day. I cried the first few mornings. But then I got mad, and now I just want to find him so I can shake him hard enough he sees sense."

A low chuckle rumbled through her father's chest. He squeezed the back of her neck, gentle but firm. "Most relationships are worth a few tears. If he's the one who makes your blood heat because you know he's smart enough to eventually admit exactly how foolish he's been"—his hand shifted, tipping her chin until he could see her eyes—"then he's worth fighting for. No halfway."

She swallowed around the knot in her throat. It made sense. It was the conclusion she'd come to.

Yet inside, fear took one more turn at winning. "What if I fight and he won't let me in?"

"Then at least you know you stood your ground." Malachi's thumb traced the line of her cheek, brushing away the dampness she hadn't noticed. "You were born stubborn, Fernie.

You were born to run toward hard things, not away from them. Don't let his fear decide your story."

She folded into him then. A brief, fierce hug that smelled of soap and flannel and home. For a heartbeat, she was small again, safe under his arm.

When she pulled back, her laugh was watery but sure. "I've still got my old goal book up in my room. Might be time to update it."

Malachi grinned, kissing her forehead. "Write it in big letters, sweetheart: *He's worth it.*"

After her dad drifted off to make another cup of tea, Fern climbed the stairs to her room. She ducked under the sloped ceiling at the side of the dormer, heart pounding for no good reason, and tugged open the bottom drawer of her oldest dresser.

There it was, buried under a stack of forgotten watercolour practice books. A cheap spiral-bound journal with *GOALS* written across the cover in purple glitter pen, letters half-rubbed away by time and too many flipped pages.

She sank cross-legged on her bed and carefully opened it.

The first few pages were painfully childish. Crooked letters declaring *Live in a castle* and *Have my own horse* to eventually *Own my own cupcake store.*

She kept turning, each page a little older, a little braver. *Get into art school. Make Mom and Dad proud. Prove I can do anything I truly want to do.*

The page turned and her lips twitched up at the sight. Her relationship goal, for whatever reasons, here it was, circled a dozen times. *Twenty-four years old. Figure out my forever person.*

A laugh hiccuped out of her, even as tears stung the corners of her eyes. Twenty-four. She'd made a goal then trusted the universe would tell her who when it was time. Destiny, she'd called it. A word that still tasted sweet on her tongue when she thought about Cody.

And *figure out* didn't just mean *find*. It meant more.

She brushed her thumb across the ink, closing her eyes for one heartbeat, two. "Guess I'm right on schedule, huh?" she whispered to the empty room.

When she looked up, her reflection in the mirror above her desk was fierce. Steady.

If Cody Gabrielle thought he could run from whatever storm he'd tangled himself in—run from her—he was about to learn exactly how stubborn Fern Fields could be.

She snapped the journal shut, stood, and squared her shoulders.

I'm ready for you, cowboy.

He wasn't supposed to be here tonight.

Hell, Cody had told himself half a dozen times on the drive back from the airport that he wouldn't set foot in her house again until he could face Fern without feeling as if he was about to split wide open.

But Chance had cornered him that afternoon at Red Boot, blocking the barn aisle like a bull moose, arms crossed. The expression in his eyes that said *big brother knows everything*.

"The Fields are gathering tonight for one of their 'we're celebrating something, but mostly we just want to get together' events. You're coming," Chance said.

Not asked, declared.

When Cody opened his mouth, Chance shook his head. "No excuses. Not this time. You need your people. And Fern— She needs you, you stubborn git. So park your pride and show up. We're picking you up so you won't be a gobshite."

Now here Cody was, boots dripping on the Fields' front doormat, the whole damn clan somewhere in the back of the house promising a warmth he didn't deserve. The smell of chili and fresh bread. The feel of home.

And Fern.

God help him, *Fern.*

She caught him dead to rights the second he stepped inside, no more dark corners or excuses. Just her standing there, one palm flat on the front door as if she'd bar the whole world from coming or going until she got her say.

He tried for casual, which was a stupid reflex. "Hey."

Not sweetheart. Not Fern. Just a damn *hey*, as if they were strangers. It made his tongue taste like ashes.

Her eyes flared.

Shit. He knew that look. He was a dead man walking.

When Rose dragged Chance toward the kitchen, Fern stepped in so close her shampoo, that faint honey-vanilla warmth that had haunted him clear across the Atlantic, hooked him in the nose and held him fast.

Fern grabbed his collar, not gently. "Upstairs. Now."

He could've joked. Could've bolted.

He didn't.

He let her steer him like a horse on a lead rope past the photo wall where little Fern grinned toothily at the camera, past the half-open doors full of family noise and safe chaos.

Up to her bedroom, tidy and bright and so very her.

When she shut the door behind them, the quiet hit him like a slap.

He braced his back against her dresser, every muscle tight. He'd faced charging cattle, ice storms, Chance's right hook when he deserved it, but none of it terrified him half as much as Fern Fields glaring at him as if she might burn him alive if he disappointed her again.

Silence fell heavy enough to bend his knees.

"You don't get to do this," Fern said. Her voice wasn't loud. Didn't need to be.

He braced a hand on the dresser, the edge digging into his back. "Fern—"

"Don't." She jabbed a finger into his chest. It landed right over his heart, and he swore the traitorous thing stumbled under her touch. "You *left*. You didn't text. You didn't call. You let me sit here in confusion, wondering what I did wrong."

"Sweetheart—"

"I *am not* your sweetheart when you treat me like an inconvenience you can put away when you feel like it." Her voice cracked. She sucked in a breath, steadying herself. "But that's not what the real problem is. Yes, I want to be your sweetheart, but you're first and foremost supposed to be my *friend*."

His chest tightened. *Oh, for fuck's sake.*

He looked away at the posters above her desk. *Dream Big. Yes You Can.* She'd scribbled a crooked heart in the corner of one of them.

We Are The Ones Who Make Our Possibilities Into Realities.

"Cody."

"You're right." The words came out astonishingly solid considering how hard he was shaking inside. Damn, he'd been so stupid. He lifted his gaze to hers. "You are my friend. Hell, you're my *best* friend, and it was shitty of me to run away like that."

"Really shitty," she agreed. The heat pouring off her faded a little.

"I'm sorry." He paused. Considered. "I didn't mean to hurt you, but I know I did. So, I'm sorry for that. For not just going back to what I know is true."

"That I'm a great listener?" Fern suggested, the hint of pitchforks and torches completely gone from her tone. "I *am* a good listener, Cody. If you need to spill whatever's got you tangled in knots, I'm here."

"Yeah." He forced the word through clenched teeth. "It's…"

For the past four weeks, he'd longed to share his worries. Yet even in Ireland with his parents, who, he knew, loved him to the core, he'd been evasive.

Now, bolstered by Fern's strength, the truth poured out of him.

"Something is physically wrong with me. I don't know yet what it is, but just the thought of not being able to do everything I want scared the hell out of me. Could be nothing. Could be…" His throat locked up. "It's stupid to drag you into that uncertainty."

Her laugh came out half sob, half wicked cackle. She stepped so close the tips of her toes bumped his. "I'm already in it, you ass. Did you think you could run off across an ocean and I'd just— What? Forget you? Stop being your friend?"

"I thought…" He shook his head, jaw tight. His hand twitched where it gripped the dresser. "I thought if it's bad you shouldn't have to deal with it."

"Stop." She cupped his face with her good hand and her short arm, both pinning him to the spot as if she would hold him up with sheer willpower. "You don't get to decide what I can handle. You don't get to protect me by ghosting me. I want *you*. As a friend. As *more* than a friend, but shove that first part into your brain hard. Friends *stick*. Even if you're scared. *Especially* then."

He wanted to promise her something easy. *It'll be fine, I'm fine.* But he couldn't lie to her. Not anymore.

So he gave her the only thing he could, the truth in the

tremor of his hand, the ache in his chest, the way he leaned into her touch like he'd been starving for it.

All true.

"You wreck me, sweetheart," he breathed.

Her lips brushed his, soft at first, then urgent. Not *I love you*, not yet, but *I want you. I choose you.*

When they broke apart, foreheads pressed together, her whisper made his eyes burn. "No more running, cowboy."

He let out a shaky laugh and felt the fight drain out of him at last. "Not unless you're chasing me."

Her smile was fierce and so damn sure. "Try me."

He kissed her again, just because he could. Just because for the first time in weeks, *they* were real—flawed, terrified, but in it together.

No more hiding.

No more trying to go it alone.

10

───────

It wasn't about keeping them a secret anymore.

Hell, if she'd thought it would help, she would have climbed onto the roof of Buns and Roses and screamed the truth to the whole town.

But Cody needed something different right now. Something quieter. Something gentler. Loving someone meant meeting them where they were, not where you wished they'd be. So she gave him time.

Time, but not space. Absolutely no more of *that* bullshit.

Thursday after work, she drove out of town to Red Boot ranch. The sun had already slipped behind the ridge of the Rocky Mountains, leaving the sky dusky purple as she parked by Cody's small cabin. He'd left the porch light on the way he did now when he knew she was coming, and that tiny act of anticipation made something squeeze warm and certain in her chest.

He met her at the door, one hand braced on the frame, eyes crinkled at the corners when he smiled.

"Hey, sweetheart."

"Hey yourself, cowboy."

An edge of uncertainty lingered in the way he stepped back to let her in, but it was his right to worry, even though he was trying to move past it.

So she ignored it and refused to treat him as if he might shatter. Instead, she brushed past him and unbuttoned her coat, her fingers brushing his chest in deliberate passing.

They made supper together nearly every other night these days. Simple things, grounding things. Buttered pasta, salad with too much feta because Cody liked it, bread from the bakery she grabbed on her lunch break.

They ate at the small kitchen table, knees bumping under the wood. No music, no background noise. Just the clink of silverware and the quiet rhythm they'd started to build.

Afterward, she curled into him on the couch, one of his thick wool blankets over their legs. Cody's arm slid around her shoulders automatically, tugging her in until her cheek rested against the soft worn fabric of his shirt.

For a while, they just sat.

No words. No demands.

Finally, his thumb traced a slow line over her upper arm, and he cleared his throat.

"Chance and Rose invited us over for dinner tomorrow night."

She smiled faintly. "Rose texted me, too. I'm okay with it, but it's your call."

"I like doing things with them." Cody's voice stayed even, but his hand stilled. "Just not sure if it's going to be weird since Chance knows about this." He gestured vaguely between them. "Have you picked up any clues from Rose? Is she still in the dark?"

Fern tilted her head to study him, considering her answer. "Rose isn't the type to tease. If she'd figured it out, she probably wouldn't have said a word to Chance. She's good at protecting people's privacy."

He pressed his lips to her temple, soft and sure in a way that still made her chest ache. "You should tell her."

"What?" She reared back slightly, mock scandalized. "Break the rules of our bet? Never."

He chuckled, but his eyes were warm. "Technically, I think I won the bet. No one knew by the end of September, but Chance had definitely figured it out in December."

"Fine, you won," she informed him primly. "But to not make it awkward, I'll put out some feelers. See what my sister does or doesn't know."

"Tansy and Ivy too," he added, all calm practicality.

Fern blinked. "You want me to spill to the whole family? Cody, Tansy is so distracted she wouldn't notice if I moved to Peru. She's got a new relationship. She's hip deep running the food situation at High Water. She can barely remember where she left her phone."

"And Ivy?"

"That's just opening the floodgates," Fern muttered. "If I tell Ivy, she'll tell Walker, who will tell his family, who are somehow related to or connected with half the town. That door can stay shut for a little longer."

Cody's brows knit together. "You're sure this isn't going to cause hurt feelings?"

"Nope." She cupped his jaw, letting her thumb stroke the rough line of stubble. "I might get teased, but teasing in six months versus teasing now... It's a win in my books."

He leaned in to kiss her, soft and slow, like they were both remembering how good this was when it was simple.

Fern pulled back just enough to unlock her phone and fire off a text to Rose

> Fern: Can I bring a date tomorrow night?

The typing dots appeared instantly.

> Rose: That's why we told you to bring Cody,
> silly girl.

Fern huffed a laugh, showing Cody the screen. "Well, that answers that question."

He exhaled. "She knew?"

Fern's phone buzzed again.

> Rose: Chance can't keep a secret to save his
> life. Once he started acting suspicious, it
> wasn't hard to guess. But don't worry. No one
> else knows unless you want them to.

Fern felt something unspool in her chest. Relief she hadn't realized she was carrying. "So much for stealth mode."

Cody still looked worried. "I don't care who knows anymore. As long as you're okay with it."

She settled in closer, pressing her lips to the underside of his jaw. "I'm better than okay."

They arrived at Rose and Chance's place the next evening just after six.

Fern loved their house. It backed right onto her mom and dad's yard. She'd grown up watching the big willow trees in the back sway over both properties as if they belonged to everyone.

The porch light glowed a welcome. She followed Cody up the steps, her heart a ridiculous combination of steady and nervous.

Rose met them at the door with a knowing smile. She hugged Fern first, then turned to Cody with that same soft affection she gave everyone she'd pulled into her wide circle of family.

"Come in, you two." She pretended not to notice how Cody hovered closer to Fern's side than usual. "Dinner's almost ready. Chance is in the kitchen insisting he's making the world's best mashed potatoes."

"Bold claim," Fern teased as they stepped farther in.

Chance popped his head around the corner, wooden spoon in hand. "I heard that!"

They all laughed, and just like that, the tension eased.

Dinner was simple and perfect. Roast beef, fluffy rolls, gravy that Fern could have happily bathed in. The potatoes that were astonishingly good. They ate around the big table, Chance and Cody telling stories about each other and growing up, Rose smiling so fondly it made Fern's chest go warm.

They didn't mention the weeks Cody had been gone, except for Rose's soft observation that she was glad he was taking care of himself.

Cody, in turn, didn't flinch when she said it.

After the plates were cleared, Chance pulled a Crokinole board out of the hall closet, setting it on the octagonal table in the den.

Cody whistled softly then rubbed his hands together. "God, I haven't played in years."

"Don't worry. We won't lose, despite your lack of skill." Fern offered a cheesy grin, sensing the spark of mischief in him that she'd missed so much.

He arched a brow. "You think you're better than me?"

"I know so."

Chance snickered. "Bro, that's just a demand for us men to take down the ladies. Gently, of course."

Rose arched a brow. "Et tu, Brute?"

He raised his hands into a what-can-I-do position. "We'll kiss it all better once you lose."

Fern and Rose exchanged evil grins. "Time to wipe the floor with them?" Fern asked.

"They asked for it," Rose pointed out. "Poor, poor suckers."

He should have known the second Chance pulled out the Crokinole board that they were doomed.

It wasn't that Cody was bad at the game, because he wasn't, but it was impossible to concentrate when Fern sat beside him, her cheeks flushed from laughter, her hair all tumbling curls bouncing around her shoulders.

He'd missed this, missed her, more than he'd let himself admit even when he was thousands of miles away pretending he could outrun whatever waited in his bones.

But running hadn't solved a damn thing. Now here he was, flicking wooden disks across the board, pretending his hands weren't liable to betray him at any second.

Fern caught his eye as Rose leaned over the table to line up her shot, and the slow grin she gave him nearly undid him. She looked so damn sure, so solid. As if she was right where she was meant to be.

As if maybe he was, too.

Chance whistled, low and sharp. "Quit making googly eyes at your girlfriend, bro, and take your turn."

Girlfriend. Even the innocent word in an innocent setting made his heart swell. "From what I see, making googly eyes at our women is a requirement for the men at this table," Cody teased back.

Fern hummed innocently as she repositioned one of the scoring pegs. "It's fine. We'll allow it. Especially if you keep losing graciously."

"Oh, sweetheart, you're in for a rude awakening." Cody flicked his disk—dead on, center hole.

It *thunked* home, and Rose gasped.

Chance whooped. "Hot damn! Look at that!"

Fern clutched her chest dramatically. "Betrayal! You've been practicing in secret."

Cody leaned back in his chair, tried to look modest and probably failed. "Just talent, sweetheart. Natural-born."

She stuck out her tongue.

Rose reached over, though, and offered him a high five. "I hate to say it, but that was beautiful."

The game settled into an easy rhythm. Bickering and cheering, the four of them slipping into that comfortable space Cody hadn't realized he'd been starving to experience again. It felt good, like coming home to himself.

As if remembering who he'd been before the fear had crawled into his gut and made him someone who ran instead of staying to fight.

It didn't escape him that this type of game, one requiring dexterity and coordination, he might not be able to play forever. The idea scared him even as it kept his ass right there in the chair, playing.

If he only had a limited time, he'd better enjoy it while he could.

By the time Rose and Fern landed their last shots, the ladies were ahead by exactly ten points. Enough to crow about for the next month.

Chance groaned. "You realize they're never going to let this go."

Fern fluttered her lashes. "Victory tastes sweeter when it's shared with family."

"You two are monsters," Chance declared, but he leaned

over and pressed a kiss to Rose's cheek, whispering something in her ear that made Rose's eyes shine.

Cody's throat went tight watching them. Simple happiness. No big declaration, no show. Just...belonging.

He wanted that. Someday.

Fern softly nudged his knee under the table. When he looked over, she gave him the smallest nod, as if she'd read every thought in his head.

Maybe she had.

After everything was cleared away, Cody stood to stretch. "I'll walk you home."

Fern tilted her head. "Sure?"

"Yeah." He looked to Rose. "Thanks for the invite."

"You're welcome anytime," Rose said softly, her gaze warm but perceptive. As if she understood exactly how hard it had been to show up tonight.

Chance clapped him on the shoulder. "Don't be a stranger."

"I won't." This time, Cody meant it.

They stepped out the back door together, boots crunching on the path between the yards. Moonlight silvered the fences and the brittle stalks of last year's perennials. The air was sharp enough to bite his lungs, but Fern's gloved hand slipped into his, and happiness warmed him deep inside.

When they reached her porch, she paused. "You okay?"

He nodded. "Better now."

"Good." She touched his cheek, her mittened hand clumsy but perfect. "You can tell me when you're not."

"I'm working on it," he admitted.

"Work faster," she teased.

Then she kissed him. Soft. With heat behind it, but mostly warmth. Comfort. A promise.

It wasn't the kind of kiss that knocked the world off its axis, but the kind that reminded him the ground was still there.

When she pulled back, she smiled up at him. "Night, cowboy."

"Night, sweetheart."

The door swung open behind her, and Malachi Fields appeared, taking in the scene with a raised brow. "Everything all right out here?"

"Just fine," Fern informed him.

"Good." He glanced between the two of them, gestured to the room behind him. "Inside is that way, kiddo."

Fern shot her dad a look. "Behave."

"I always do," Malachi said blandly, stepping aside to let her pass.

Fern slipped into the house, but she glanced back and blew Cody a final kiss. The expression in her eyes so sweet and trusting, he just stood there and breathed deep.

No matter what, tonight was going to be okay.

Malachi gestured to the snow-dusted chairs on the patio. "You got time to sit?"

Cody hesitated then nodded. "Yeah. I'd like that."

They settled side by side, breath fogging the cold air. For a long minute, neither spoke. The moon hung low over the neighbouring roofs, and somewhere down the street a dog barked, a thin lonely sound.

Malachi cleared his throat. "Fern's been stubborn since the day she was born."

Cody huffed out a laugh. "I've noticed that hasn't changed much."

"But she's also loyal. She doesn't give up on the people she cares about." Malachi shifted, turning just enough to meet Cody's gaze. "You're a lucky man."

Cody swallowed, his voice suddenly rough. "I know."

"Friendship is a fine foundation," Malachi continued. "Stronger than a lot of folks realize. And you two...you've built something good there."

"I hope so." Cody drew in a slow breath. "I want more. Someday. But right now, I'm just trying to figure out how to stop screwing up."

Malachi's chuckle was low, warm. "We all screw up. Over and over again. The trick isn't pretending you won't, it's learning to get back up and mean it when you say you're sorry." He paused. "Learning how to share what you don't know yet. Women in particular like that. It's less about the details and more about feelings, which we men sometimes fail to deliver."

Cody looked down at his hands. He flexed them slowly and tried to ignore the way the left one trembled. "I've got a referral to a neurologist in Calgary. Mid-February."

Malachi nodded, nothing but understanding on his lined face. "Good. Once you know more, you'll know more. Until then, you let the people who care about you stand beside you when you want, and you tell them when you need room to breathe—but tell them, either way."

Cody swallowed hard. "I'm trying."

"You are now, and that's good to see." Malachi stood, waited until Cody joined him, then squeezed his shoulder. "Better than good, son."

The word lodged in Cody's chest, bright and painful and perfect. *Son.* The word, from a man who's opinion mattered, meant the world.

"Thank you," he managed.

"You're welcome." Malachi stepped back inside, leaving Cody alone with the night.

For a moment, Cody just breathed. Let himself feel the cold, the quiet, the relief that maybe, just maybe, he hadn't broken everything that mattered.

His phone buzzed in his pocket.

> Fern: Text me when you get home. I worry.

He smiled, thumb hovering over the keys.

> Cody: I will.

After a heartbeat, he added:

> Cody: I don't know if I want you at that appointment yet. The one in February. I might need to do it by myself.

Three dots flickered.

> Fern: That's okay. Just promise you'll tell me what happens when you're ready.

> Cody: I promise.

When he finally turned to walk back across the yard to his truck, the fear was still there, gnawing at the edges of his thoughts. But fear wasn't the only thing.

Because for the first time in a long time, he *knew* he wasn't walking alone.

11

———————

Fern leaned back on the smooth wooden bench and tilted her head toward the steel beams and sparkling windows arching high above them. Greenery dripped from every ledge, ferns and orchids lush against glass walls that let the February sun flood the Devonian Gardens in Calgary.

"I am officially shopped out," she declared to the rafters.

Rose, perched cross-legged beside her with a reusable shopping bag full of pottery finds, pressed a hand to her heart. "Blasphemy."

Tansy huffed, hauling another bag onto the floor to make room to stretch out on the wide bench. "It's been an amazing trip, though. You have to admit I hit gold with this whisk. Look at the handle. It's ergonomic porn."

Fern groaned. "You and your kitchen gadgets."

"She's a diva," Rose agreed gravely. "And not even sorry about it."

"Zero regret," Tansy confirmed, her smile smug. "Once I replace the last of the thrift store utensils in the High Water kitchen, I will ascend to my final form, Goddess of All Things Delicious."

Fern laughed so hard she nearly toppled off the bench.

Rose's phone pinged with an alert. "Okay, we've got about thirty minutes before my next appointment with a distributor. Ten minutes, if we really want to keep going."

"I do not," Fern said firmly. She stretched her legs in front of her and closed her eyes, letting the warmth from the skylights soak into her bones. "I'm staying right here with my sore feet and my excellent mood."

Tansy leaned her shoulder against hers. "You sure you're not just waiting for a *secret admirer* to text you?"

Fern cracked one eye open. "A secret admirer?"

"Yes," Tansy said solemnly. "The one who probably follows you around Buns and Roses, pining after you."

Rose snorted. "You read too many romance novels."

Tansy shrugged. "Or maybe you're waiting to hear from Cody. Honestly, I can't figure out why you two haven't just moved in together. You're practically joined at the hip."

Fern's pulse jumped, but she schooled her face into amusement. "Really?"

"I know, I know. You're *friends*." Tansy waved a dismissive hand. "But I swear it's like you two went back to elementary school and are now doing all the super cute *friends forever* things, quote unquote. Like make up a secret language and a secret handshake. If he ever needs a reference for his next girlfriend, he can tell her he's got the *Fern Fields stamp of approval*."

Rose smothered a smile and bent to examine her coffee lid, not commenting. Fern sent her a look, and Rose's mouth twitched. She was definitely not going to confirm anything.

"Are you quite done analyzing my *friend?*" Fern asked.

"For now." Tansy sighed dramatically. "You need to start

hanging around more other unattached cowboys so I have fodder for speculation."

Fern opened her mouth—and then her phone buzzed in her pocket.

Speak of the devil.

She pulled it out, already smiling.

> Cody: How's the get away?

> Fern: Sister-filled and glorious. But I miss you.

The typing dots popped up immediately.

> Cody: Miss you too, sweetheart.

Her heart did a little flip. After everything they'd gone through, after Ireland, after January, he made her feel as if someone had cracked her ribs open and tucked something warm and precious right against her heart.

Another bubble popped up.

> Cody: Also…I have a favour to ask.

She straightened. "Hang on, girls."

Three dots blinked, then vanished. Reappeared. She waited, thumb hovering.

> Cody: My appointment for testing got moved up. It's tomorrow. I know you're with your sisters, but…

The dots paused. Fern's chest squeezed.

> Cody: You feel like sitting in boring reception rooms so I can hug you when the bullshit's over? I'll buy you dinner on the way home.

She didn't hesitate.

> Fern: Yes. Absolutely yes.

> Cody: You sure? You don't have to.

> Fern: I WANT to.

She looked up to find Rose watching her knowingly while Tansy was blissfully preoccupied digging in her tote for a protein bar.

"Potential change of plans if you guys don't mind," Fern said carefully. "Cody's going to be in town tomorrow. If you can drop me off at around ten, I'll spend the day with him then we'll ride home together."

Rose's brows arched then she looked away, expression smooth as glass.

Tansy popped her head back up, looking delighted. "Oh, fun. A Cody day. Convince him to buy some decent jeans. I swear he's been wearing the same pair since last fall."

Fern coughed to cover her laugh. "I think he has more than one pair."

"You're enabling him." Tansy pointed accusingly. "I know wardrobe minimalism is a thing, but you're a bad influence."

Rose cleared her throat delicately. "Or a good one," she murmured.

Fern shot her a look that said *don't you dare.*

Rose just raised an innocent brow and sipped her coffee.

Tansy, oblivious, stretched out her legs. "Well, tell Cody hi for me. And that if he ever wants to offer me a prize, I'm game—

since *someone*—" she jabbed a dramatic thumb into her chest, "arranged and then graciously bowed out of the trail ride that was the start of the epic friendship between you two."

Fern clutched her chest. "Are you still going on about that?"

"Yes," Tansy deadpanned. "I am."

Rose laughed quietly. "She's never going to let that go."

"Never," Tansy confirmed cheerfully.

Saturday morning was bright with that clear, deceptive light that made the sidewalks look warm instead of brittle and minus twenty.

Fern hugged her sisters tightly on the curb outside the café where Cody said he'd meet her.

"You want us to stay?" Rose asked softly, her hand on Fern's shoulder.

Fern shook her head. "No. I'm good."

"Have fun." Tansy kissed her cheek. "Text us later. And don't let him skip lunch. Cowboys are the worst."

"I won't."

Fern waved them off then turned toward the café entrance just in time to see Cody step through the door. His eyes landed on her and softened instantly.

"Hey," he murmured.

"Hey yourself." She leaned in for a hug, and he clung to her briefly, the hold tight and needy.

"You ready?" she asked softly when they pulled apart.

He swallowed, that flicker of vulnerability she'd come to recognize crossing his face. "I don't know."

She cupped his jaw, brushing her thumb over the faint stubble on his cheek. "That's okay. I am."

For a moment, he looked as if he was memorizing her face before nodding. "All right. Let's go."

The waiting rooms were just as dull and sterile as she'd

imagined. Grey chairs, a looping slideshow of nature programs on one overhead screen, news on another.

Fern ignored both and held Cody's hand until he was called for his MRI and the clinical neurological exam. She kissed his cheek when he looked as if he might bolt and offered her best encouraging smile.

When he came out, hours later, pale and exhausted but standing, she rose and wrapped her arms around him without a word. His breath shuddered against her hair, but he didn't pull away.

When he finally spoke, his voice was rough when he said, "Thanks for being here."

She tipped her head back. "Always."

"Even when it's ugly?"

"Especially then."

He kissed her. Just a brush of lips, but it steadied them both. She tucked her arm through his and leaned against him as they walked into the bright afternoon.

They didn't know yet what came next. But they were going to find out.

Together.

Cody hadn't realized how much he'd been counting on answers, real answers, until he walked out of Dr. Sydney Jeremiah's office in Heart Falls in mid-March with nothing to show but another requisition form.

More tests. More waiting.

He kept the paper folded in his back pocket all afternoon. Didn't even look at it until he was alone, sitting in his truck in the Red Boot parking lot with the engine ticking as it cooled. He laid the slip on his thigh and read every word twice, as if memorizing the medical code numbers would somehow feel like progress instead of spinning in place.

It didn't.

He scrubbed a hand over his jaw, feeling the scruff because today he hadn't managed to shave, and let his head fall back against the seat. Outside, the early spring wind picked at the eaves and sent a loose scrap of feed bag skittering across the gravel. In the last light of the day, it looked almost alive.

He didn't want to bring the heaviness home to Fern. She deserved better than his half-exhausted silences. But he'd promised to try, so he did.

It was hard, but he told her the truth.

"It was inconclusive," he said that night when she stopped by with a bag of takeout and the determination to make him eat something. "More tests coming. I don't know when it'll end."

Fern sat beside him on the couch and took his hand. "Then we wait," she said simply, squeezing until he felt the tremor in his knuckles ease a fraction. "Together."

The days blurred, a quiet rhythm of work and trying not to think too hard.

The only thing that broke the monotony was Karen waving him down by the main paddock one morning, her cheeks pink from the cold.

"You got a sec?" she called, voice bright.

"Sure." He leaned on the railing, tucking the schedule in his hand away in a pocket. "What's up?"

Her smile was incandescent. He'd never seen Karen look as if she might burst with happiness. "I'm expecting."

It took him a second to understand, then he blinked, his brows shooting up. "You—*really?*"

"Finn and I found out a few weeks ago. I wanted to wait until the first ultrasound before telling folks." She bit her lip.

"It'll mean a lot more for you to pick up when I'm farther along."

He was still grappling with the surprise, and the pang of envy that surprised him even more. *They knew their future,* he thought numbly. He didn't even know if he'd be able to button his damn shirt in a year.

But he forced the bitterness aside and reached across to squeeze her shoulder. "Congratulations, Karen. That's... honestly, that's wonderful news."

Relief crossed her face. "Thank you. You'll let me know what you can take on? If you'd rather not pick up extra long-term, I completely understand, and we'll look at hiring."

"I'll look at the schedule," he promised. "Short-term, don't worry about a thing. I'll cover it."

When she left, he took a minute before moving again. Let himself lean into the wind, his breath steaming out ragged and cold.

Late March blurred into April. He did his best to show up. For Karen. For the ranch. For Fern, most of all. It wasn't easy, but somehow pushing to be there for them meant he found strength he didn't know he had.

Not every day, but often enough.

The night before Rose and Tansy's joint birthday party, he lay awake in bed, staring at the plank ceiling of his cabin, listening to the ghosts of his doubts scuffle around in the dark.

He didn't know how to need someone so intensely. But Fern never stopped offering to catch him when he fell. Accepting that was slowly getting easier.

On the day of the party, he almost didn't go. He'd been in the barn all morning, fixing a gate hinge he could have replaced twice over on a good day.

Today was not a good day. Not only because of his hand, but because he kept thinking about the inconclusive report.

Somehow, she knew. Fern texted midafternoon.

> Fern: Don't you dare chicken out.
>
> Fern: I'll meet you at four. It's not fancy, it's family. Remember that.

So he showed up.

She stood on the porch, smiling as if he was exactly what she'd been waiting for, and he forgot to be afraid. Forgot to be worried and tired and lost.

He reached for her hand automatically, and she laced her fingers through his without hesitation. That single touch steadied something deep in his chest.

"Hey," he murmured.

"Hey yourself, cowboy," she said, her smile soft. "You okay?"

He nodded then ducked to press a kiss to her hair. "Better now."

Inside, the Fields family was exactly what he needed even though they were everything he feared. So many people, with so many watchful eyes.

But they were also kind, and careful not to prod. They knew he was dealing with medical stuff and somehow stayed supportive without being invasive.

A lot of them still hadn't clued in that he and Fern were more than friends, which was amusing in an entirely different way.

It was nearly sunset when he slipped out back, needing a breath of air. The late April sky was a wash of lavender and gold. Carter was laughing somewhere behind the house, and the low drone of Walker's guitar carried into the cool night.

Along with Fern's voice, calling his name from the porch.

"Hey," she said softly, stepping down to meet him. "You okay?"

He nodded, swallowing past the knot in his throat. "Just... needed a minute."

She looked at him for a long moment, then turned her head toward Rose and Chance's place across the adjoining yard. "Want to go sit for a bit? Somewhere quieter?"

It was all the invitation he needed.

He followed her across the grass, through the side gate, and up the back steps of Rose and Chance's house. Inside, it was quiet with everyone over at the other house. Fern tugged him down the hall to the little guest room tucked behind the kitchen.

The second the door closed his restraint snapped.

He caught her around the waist and kissed her so hard she made a startled, muffled sound against his mouth. She wound her arms around his shoulders and kissed him back, fierce and sure. When he pulled back, he was breathing ragged.

"Christ, sweetheart. You undo me."

She traced fingers down his jaw, her eyes dark with heat. "Good."

He kissed her again. Softer this time, but no less urgent. His hands skimmed down to the small of her back, her hips, the sweet curve he'd thought about more nights than he could count.

"You want this?" he whispered.

Her answering nod was the surest thing he'd ever seen.

He backed her against the wall, stopping only long enough to brush his thumb over her cheekbone, to memorize the way she looked right then.

Flushed and certain and beautiful.

Then he kissed her again, and the rest of the world fell away.

12

---

*S*he should have been embarrassed by how fast she went from heated kisses to desperate need. But God, with Cody, there was no shame, only that delicious ache blooming low in her belly as he hauled her tighter, his mouth never leaving hers.

When he pressed her back against the wall of Rose and Chance's guestroom, somewhere between *just need you* and *can't wait another second*, Fern clutched his shoulders as if they were the only solid thing in the universe. His hands skimmed under the hem of her dress, callused palms rough on her thighs, and she nearly whimpered.

"Doing this?" he murmured against her mouth, his voice ragged, "Is going to get us caught."

"Only if you don't *hurry*."

His grin was pure wickedness as she arched into his touch.

He huffed a laugh, the sound turning into a groan as she slipped a hand between them, cupping him through his jeans. Hard, hot— God, she'd been thinking about this all week. She pressed her cheek to his and whispered, "I promise not to use my prosthesis on any of your delicate bits."

His breath caught. "You're evil."

"You like me that way." She popped the button on his fly with her right hand—her sure, nimble hand—and wrapped her fingers around him. The way he shuddered, the way he buried his face against her neck and bit gently at her collarbone, nearly undid her.

She stroked him slow, savouring every ragged gasp, every tremor. His hand braced on the wall beside her head, fingers curling tight in her hair. They were already half-wild, her panties pushed aside, the hem of her dress rucked up around her hips. She could feel how close he was. His breath hitched, his hips jerking into her hand.

"Fuck, *Fern*—" He tried to pull away, but she sank to her knees before he could stop her. His startled, desperate noise went straight to her core.

"Sweetheart, don't—"

"Oh, I'm going to," she promised, all satin and sin. She met his eyes as she licked the head of his cock, just a teasing swirl of her tongue, and his jaw locked.

She loved that. Loved undoing the calm he tried so hard to hold onto.

When she took him deeper, his thighs tensed under her palm. His hand tangled in her hair, not forcing, just holding on as if he'd fly apart without the anchor. She worked him slow, savouring the taste, the heat, the helpless sounds he couldn't bite back.

He tried to warn her, she knew he did. His hand flexed against her cheek, his hips twitching. But before he could finish the words, he made a broken noise and pulled her up. His mouth crashed into hers, and she tasted salt and heat and him.

"Not like that," he growled against her lips. "I need to be inside you."

Her whole body lit up in response. "Then do it."

He spun her, pressing her forearms to the wall, angling her hips out and up. He pushed her dress higher, and she felt the heat of him as he knocked her feet apart.

"Tell me if it's too much," he rasped.

"Try me." She twisted her head just enough to watch as he covered himself with a condom. Then their eyes met, and whatever restraint he'd been clinging to shattered.

When he pressed into her, she bit her lip to keep from crying out. He filled her in a slow, unhurried yet unstoppable thrust, and her whole body went tight. He stayed still, forehead resting between her shoulder blades, breath ragged.

"Christ," he whispered. "You feel... *God.*"

"Move," she demanded, every nerve ending on fire. "Please."

He obeyed, and it wasn't sweet anymore. It was hard and hungry and exactly what she'd needed. He pushed her hard, and she surged upward until her cheek pressed to the cool wall as he drove into her. Her whole body went liquid under the force of it. His hands locked on her hips, body curled over her, and something about the way he held her so securely made her heart feel just as exposed as her body.

"Cody—" She tried to say something else, but all that came out was a keening gasp as her climax tore through her.

He groaned her name into her hair, hips stuttering as he followed her over the edge.

For a long moment, they just stayed there. Her pinned to the wall, him pressed against her back, their breathing ragged and tangled together.

Then her phone buzzed from her discarded jacket on the floor. A second later, Cody's pocket chimed too.

He dropped a kiss to her neck, voice rough with spent desire. "That's definitely Chance. Bet you ten bucks he's warning us the cake is about to be cut."

Fern let out a strangled laugh. "God, our family is going to kill us."

"Not if we sneak back quick as if nothing happened." He eased out of her, hands gentle as he tugged her dress back into place. "We can do innocent."

She turned, feeling deliciously wrecked, and kissed him softly. "We're terrible at innocent."

He smirked. "Worth it."

They scrambled to make themselves look presentable. Her hair was a mass of hopeless tangles, but she did her best to tease it into submission. Cody dealt with the condom then tucked himself away, glancing around and looking for things to straighten up as he zipped his jeans.

"Okay," she panted, checking her reflection in the little mirror by the door. "We have about thirty seconds to look like we haven't been—"

He kissed her again, slow and sweet, and she melted despite herself.

When they stepped back into the yard at her parents, Rose arched an eyebrow that said *I know exactly what you two were doing.*

Fern pasted on her sweetest smile.

A chorus of voices started singing "Happy Birthday," and she and Cody slipped in beside Tansy, who, thankfully, was very distracted by the cake.

More and more people knew about them, but somehow having Tansy in the dark was extra delightful.

Fern got through the rest of the celebration without giving herself away, but every time Cody's hand brushed hers, she felt it again. A promise humming between them.

Two weeks later on May first, bright and early the morning of her twenty-fourth birthday, she opened the door to find him standing there with a bouquet of roses and that crooked smile that made her knees go loose.

"Happy birthday, sweetheart." He kissed her slow, the kind of kiss that made her forget her own name.

She pulled back, grinning. "Thanks. You're forgiven for being so early because the flowers are amazing."

"You're even more beautiful," he said before hurrying on. "But I do have an apology. I need to head out of town for a couple days. There are a couple of horses to pick up in Yorkton." Her heart dipped, but before she could tell him it was okay, he added, "Come with me."

She blinked. "What?"

"Come with me," he repeated. "We'll get the horses, have a nice meal, stay somewhere that isn't a teeny cabin at the place I work. Just you and me time."

She squealed, flinging her arms around his neck. "Give me fifteen minutes!"

She was halfway down the hall before he called after her. "Don't forget your swimsuit!"

Fern grinned so hard her cheeks ached. This was going to be the Best. Birthday. Ever.

HE'D BARELY HAD time to admire her rapidly retreating figure flying up the stairs before Sophie Fields appeared in the archway to the left of the foyer. Arms folded, one brow cocked, she appeared to have been waiting there the whole time, ready to pounce.

"Kidnapping my daughter, are you?" she asked, her voice sweet enough to make the hair on the back of his neck stand up.

Cody pasted on his most harmless expression. "Just taking her out for a nice dinner. And a getaway," he added honestly, transferring the roses from one hand to another.

"A nice dinner," Malachi repeated as he also stepped into the foyer. His mouth curved in a sly smile. "In another province?" Cody opened his mouth to explain, but Malachi winked. "Must be quite the restaurant."

Damn. Cody lost his amusement. "I'm not messing up any birthday plans, am I? I didn't think there was a family gathering tonight or anything."

"No, no," Malachi assured him, waving a hand. "There are a few other concerns keeping the extended family busy right now, so it was just going to be Fern and us. You're welcome to take care of our girl."

Sophie swung a finger at him, but Cody didn't miss the smile tugging at her lips. "Let her take care of you. Lord knows she's determined to."

"I'm nearly ready!" Fern's voice floated down the staircase.

"Let me take those," Sophie ordered, reaching for the bouquet. "They're gorgeous."

"Rose said they were Fern's favourite," Cody admitted.

"They are, but I doubt you have room to take them with you. I'll put them in water and they'll still be perfect when you're back," Sophie assured him.

Fern reappeared a moment later, overnight bag slung over her shoulder, her other hand braced lightly on the banister. Her cheeks were flushed, but her eyes met Cody's with a glint that made his chest feel too small. As if she'd take on the whole damn world if it tried to get in their way.

She spotted her parents and grinned. "I get a birthday getaway."

"You deserve one," her mom said. "I'll deal with your flowers."

"We'll celebrate when you're back," Malachi promised. "Drive safe."

"Thanks, Mom. Thanks, Dad."

Cody took the bag from her. Fern gave her parents each a quick hug then stepped past them to Cody's side, her expression bright with anticipation.

"Let's go."

Just like that, he couldn't imagine being anywhere else.

It felt natural. Too natural. As if he'd spent half his life waiting for this. Her smile, her trust, her warmth, and had only just found it.

He opened her door, and she slid into the passenger seat. "I'll do a search for the perfect first coffee stop. Plus, I'm determined to win our roadside trivia game. Just wait and see."

Sliding behind the wheel, his lungs felt clear for the first time in weeks.

He could do this. For one day, he could pretend nothing was wrong.

The road stretched out in front of them. Kilometer after kilometer of highway, a black ribbon gleaming in the spring sun. They talked the whole damn way. Ten hours, and somehow they never ran out of things to say.

Fern read him her birthday texts as they rolled in, every one of them making her smile that much brighter.

"Charity says surprise getaways are the best," she announced as they passed through Swift Current. "And that I should ask for riding lessons."

Cody snorted. "You're already a good rider."

"I think she's remembering her own surprise escape. She also says, and I quote—'tell your ridiculously hot not-boyfriend that if he fails to find you birthday pie, he's dead to me.'" Fern tilted the phone so he could see the winking emoji. "Any rebuttal?"

"Only that I'm not sure whether to be offended that she thinks I can't find you pie or flattered at the hot comment."

Fern snickered. "Here's from Rose. She says, 'Hope you're having a perfect day, and that you know how lucky you are.'"

Heat prickled under his collar, but he kept his eyes on the road. "Pretty sure I'm the lucky one."

The silence that followed was soft and golden. She reached across her body and laid her hand on his thigh, her thumb stroking little circles as if she knew exactly how to quiet the noise in his head.

When Tansy's message came through, Fern cracked up so hard she had to wipe tears off her cheeks before she could read it aloud.

"Oh, this is golden," she gasped, voice wobbly with laughter. "Tansy says—'Seriously, this is why I'm jealous you have Cody. Best platonic guy friend ever. Who else would drive you to another province on your birthday? Buy that man a sandwich.'"

Cody barked out a laugh, his chest going tight in the best way. "She really has no clue, does she?"

"Not even a little." Fern shook her head, still giggling. "God, she's going to feel so silly when she figures it out."

"Or smug," he pointed out. "She might act as if she knew all along."

She gave him a look, all dry amusement. "She's not that good an actress."

Dinner in Yorkton was better than he'd dared hope. Just the two of them in a little restaurant that smelled like roasted garlic and fresh bread. They both ordered steak, and Fern enthusiastically matched him bite for bite.

"You're beyond pretty," he said as she dabbed sauce from her lip. "But I think the fact you can eat like a lumberjack makes me even hotter."

Her foot nudged his under the table. "Stop it."

Not likely.

Later, when they walked back to the hotel, the night air was cool and clean. Fern looped her arm through his, leaning her head briefly on his shoulder. He wished the moment could stretch on forever, the simple sweetness of being hers.

The hotel pool was nearly empty, and for once, he didn't feel self-conscious about the faint tremor in his hand. Not with Fern floating close, her leg brushing his as they drifted together in the warm water.

"Don't you dare start worrying," she said, her voice soft as her fingers slid over his wrist. "Not tonight."

He swallowed. "I'm not."

She raised a brow. "Liar."

He didn't have a comeback because she was right. He was always worrying about something. The test results, the future, about what she'd have to carry if things turned out the way he feared.

But when she kissed him, none of it mattered. Not for those precious seconds.

When they finally tumbled into bed, her hair a dark halo on the pillow, her hands tugging him down, he let himself stop thinking altogether.

It wasn't rushed, or clumsy, or full of desperation this time. It was slow, deliberate, and so good it almost broke him apart. She gasped when he pressed into her, pleasure a whisper against his mouth.

He moved over her in long, unhurried strokes, savouring every sigh, every soft cry, every time her nails bit into his shoulders. She was so beautiful like this. Unguarded, trusting him with all of it.

For a while, it was easy to forget that anything waited beyond this room.

After, she curled into his side, her cheek pressed over his heart. He traced lazy patterns on her back, breathing her in, memorizing the feel of her.

It should have been perfect. It *was* perfect.

But the minute her breathing evened out in sleep, the thoughts came crawling back, cold and sharp.

She deserves this every day. This peace, this joy. Not a man who might lose pieces of himself.

He examined his hand where it rested on her hip. The fingers that sometimes didn't listen to him anymore, and his chest went tight.

What if I can't give her this for the long haul? What if the best thing I can do for her is to let her go before she's too far in to walk away?

Fern shifted in her sleep, a soft little sigh as she burrowed closer and held him tighter. As if she could feel his doubt and was determined to chase it away even in her dreams.

He closed his eyes and rested his cheek against her hair.

Tomorrow, he'd find a way to believe he was enough. For tonight, he'd let himself be hers.

Just hers.

13

___

$\mathcal{H}$e'd been thinking about this the wrong way, Cody decided. Maybe the trick wasn't to wait for answers but to pretend he didn't need them. If he didn't know what was wrong, he could pretend nothing was. He could carry on, work, ride, be with Fern, and it could all be enough.

But when the specialist's office called him in the second Thursday in June, even the trees budding along the Glenbow Clinic parking lot couldn't fool him into hoping. Spring was wasted on him.

The doctor's office smelled like lemon cleaner and the strong tang of anxiety—his own. He sat across from her desk, hands folded tight in his lap, willing them to stay still.

She didn't drag it out. Maybe he was grateful for that.

"Cody." Dr. Jorgenson's voice was calm, not gentle exactly, but direct in a way he'd come to respect. "We have your results. I want to be clear—we don't assign a diagnosis lightly. But based on your history, exam, and the imaging we did, you have what we call young-onset Parkinson's disease."

The words dropped onto his chest like a stone.

"Young-onset," he repeated.

"It means you're under forty when it begins," she explained. "Which comes with different challenges but also some advantages. People your age typically respond better to medication, and they tend to stay active longer."

Cody stared at the floor, where the toe of his boot scuffed a pale mark across the tile. "And eventually?"

Her silence was just long enough to feel honest. "It's progressive. There's no cure yet. But we can manage symptoms for years, sometimes decades. You'll have good days and harder ones. It doesn't define you."

Didn't it, though? The tremor in his hand already felt like a billboard announcing his weakness.

He forced a breath and tried to joke. "Bottom line, I'm rusting early."

Dr. Jorgenson smiled. "That's one way to put it. Your brain isn't making dopamine the way it should. We'll start medication, see how you respond. How you react to the treatment often gives us more clarity than tests alone."

"My work," he said hoarsely. "I ride. I ranch. I—"

"You may need to make adjustments," she acknowledged. "At some point. But you're not powerless, Cody. You're still you. You'll still be you when you're on medication and when you need help, when you need to ask for more than you ever have."

He thought of Fern. The way she looked at him, as if he was her safe place. Her someday.

A memory flashed. Her in his passenger seat, singing along to some country station, her prosthesis resting lightly on her thigh while she tapped out the beat with her other hand. She didn't hide her difference. Didn't apologize for it.

Maybe he could learn something from her. But right now,

he couldn't feel anything but the weight pressing on his ribs, making it hard to breathe.

He left the clinic with a pamphlet crumpled in one hand and a prescription in the other. In the truck, he sat with the engine off and let the numbness crawl over him.

Parkinson's.

Not a death sentence. But a different life.

Could he give Fern what she deserved? A partner who might need care in his forties? Who might someday need help dressing, eating, riding—

His throat locked up.

That night, he couldn't face anyone. He drove past Red Boot, past the turnoff to town, kept going west until the foothills swallowed him in silence. He pulled into a gravel turnout, killed the lights, and leaned his head on the steering wheel.

This was what a coward did. Hide.

But he couldn't bring himself and his news to Fern, not until he figured out how to say the words without shattering.

It was hours before he dug out his phone. He typed the message and stared at it so long the screen dimmed and went dark. When he finally pressed Send, his thumb was trembling.

> Cody: I need a couple days to clear my head.
> Camping out west, no signal. I'll be back.
> Please don't worry.

He hesitated, then typed the last line. The truth, unvarnished.

> Cody: I love you.

It was cowardly, maybe, to say it in a text. But he couldn't choke it out in person yet, and it had to be said.

He set the phone aside and let the night come down around him, quiet and cold.

In the morning, dawn found him still awake. He climbed out of the cab, stretched, and let the wind scour some of the heaviness off his skin. If he was going to be any kind of man, any kind of partner, he couldn't hide forever.

But for a day or two, he needed to remember who he was without the label. Just Cody. A man who loved horses and early mornings and a woman who deserved everything he was afraid he couldn't give.

He'd come back. He would look her in the eye and tell her the truth.

But for now, he watched the sun climb over the hills and let himself pretend he was healthy and sound.

Just for a little while longer.

FERN READ the text three times, the words blurring as her heart crashed against her ribs.

I need a couple days to clear my head. Camping out west, no signal. I'll be back. Please don't worry.

Then, the last line.

I love you.

Her throat closed. She pressed a hand to her mouth and breathed through the tremor building in her chest. That was the first time he'd said it, *I love you.*

So why did it read like a goodbye?

She swallowed hard, willing her hands to steady enough to type.

> Fern: I'm here when you're ready. I'm here even if you're not ready.

She hit Send before she could overthink it. Then she dropped the phone onto her bed and braced her forearms on the mattress. For a moment, she just let herself feel it all. The elation of knowing he loved her, the dread that he might think he had to set her free.

No.

She wiped her cheeks and forced herself upright. There was no kindness in letting him hide from the one person who would stand beside him no matter what.

He was hers. She was his. They'd figure out the rest.

She tucked her phone in her pocket and went to work.

The gallery was quiet that day. Fern set up a new display, labeled tags, arranged pottery. Everything she'd normally enjoy. But her brain kept replaying Cody's message.

I love you.

Which she slowly figured out also meant *I'm sorry*. And *I'm scared*.

By late afternoon, she was sorting a crate of hand-carved frames when Chance walked in. He didn't say anything at first, just set a thermos of coffee on the table beside her.

She unscrewed the lid, inhaling the familiar smell. "Thanks."

"You look like you've been to war," Chance said gently.

She shrugged, not trusting her voice.

He studied her a moment longer. "Something wrong?"

Fern pressed her lips together. The truth slipped out before she could stop it. "I think Cody got a diagnosis."

Chance's jaw tightened. "He's being an eejit?"

"Maybe." She managed a small smile. "But he's my eejit. So, there's that."

Chance pulled her into a brotherly hug, his big arms bracketing her shoulders. "He'll figure it out. He won't walk away from you."

She squeezed him back. "Thanks, Chance."

When he left, she locked the door behind him and rested her forehead against the cool glass.

She knew what might be happening. She wasn't naive. She'd spent hours reading medical articles and Parkinson's forums in the dark. She'd learned more than she'd ever wanted to know about dopamine, tremors, progression.

So she thought about it. *Really* thought about it. What it meant to love someone who might someday need her help to button a shirt or tie a boot. To watch him slow down before his time.

To stand beside him when he couldn't hide it anymore.

She imagined it all. The frustration, the adjustments, the way people would look at them.

It scared her for a bit, but understanding came quick and clear.

She wasn't scared because she didn't want to deal with it, but because she didn't want *him* to have to deal with it.

The actual doing of the things? The being with Cody through it all? None of that scared her.

It was startling, the realization. So big it made her knees buckle.

She sat right there on the gallery floor and cried. Not because she was sad, though she was. Or afraid—though she felt that too. But because she knew with unshakable certainty that she loved him.

Not just him of today. The him of tomorrow, too. Every version of Cody was hers.

Just like she was his.

He came to her door on Saturday morning when she was still sitting in her pyjamas staring out the kitchen window. Her heart tried to jump out of her ribs. She pressed a hand to her chest then opened the front door.

He looked tired and worn thin around the edges. But his eyes met hers the way they always had. As if she was the only thing tethering him to earth.

"Hey," she whispered.

"Hey." His voice cracked.

She stepped back to let him in. "No one's home. They're at the bookstore."

He nodded. "Can we talk?"

"Yeah."

He tried to start right then and there, but she didn't let him. She sat on the couch and patted the spot beside her.

When he sat, his thigh trembled against hers.

He didn't start with excuses. He didn't even try to soften it.

"It's Parkinson's."

She nodded once, steady. "Okay."

"It's progressive." His jaw clenched. "There's no cure. The meds help, but someday..."

She laced her fingers through his. "Someday isn't today."

He looked down at their joined hands. "You deserve someone who can promise you stability. Someone who won't wake up one day needing help out of bed."

Her chest ached. But she kept her voice calm. "You deserve someone who won't run when things get hard."

He blew out a shaky breath. "Maybe I should go in the bachelor auction. Make a clean break. Let you off the hook."

Her laugh startled both of them. "Go for it if it makes you feel better." She lifted her chin. "It's not going to change anything between us in the long run."

His eyes snapped to hers, searching. "You mean that?"

"I do." She brushed her thumb over the back of his hand. "I can't promise it won't be hard sometimes. But I can promise I won't leave."

He looked as if he might break right there. She couldn't stand it.

"Come here."

She tugged him forward until he was between her knees. She lifted his chin, forcing him to meet her gaze.

"I choose you," she whispered. "I'll keep choosing you."

When she kissed him, it wasn't soft. It wasn't pity. It was heat and want and the fierce certainty that she would stand beside him no matter what came next.

His hands fisted on her waist as if he couldn't bear to let her go.

She pushed him to vertical then guided him up the stairs. Deliberate, intentional. A choice they were both making to be together.

Fern finally closed the door to her bedroom then eased him back onto the mattress, kissing him because she could, because she wanted to.

"You don't have to prove anything," she murmured as she unbuttoned his shirt. "You don't have to be anything but mine."

"Fern—"

"Shh." She smiled, wicked and sure. "I'm going to make you forget everything else."

So she did.

When he finally came apart under her hands, she held him close, kissing the curve of his shoulder.

Someday still scared him. Maybe it always would.

But she wasn't going anywhere.

She knew, without a doubt, he'd figure that out soon enough.

14

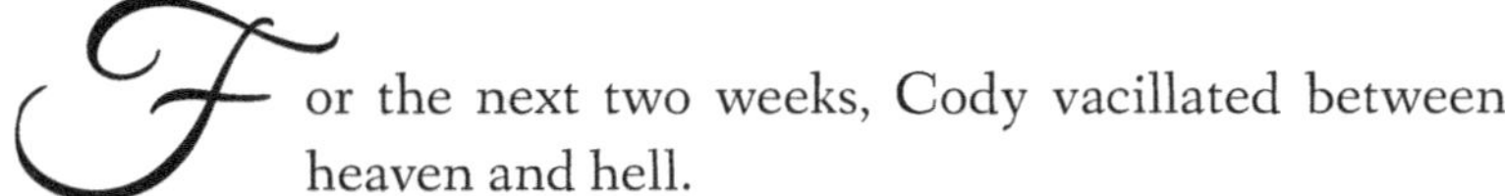

For the next two weeks, Cody vacillated between heaven and hell.

Fern loved him.

She'd said it. She'd whispered it into his hair, pressed it into his skin with her lips, texted it in the quiet hours when she thought he might need to hear it most.

Every time that bone-deep part of him quavered in believing that he was worthy of her, he made sure to say it back, and every time it meant something more.

I love you. *I care so much.*

I love you. *I'm afraid, but you being there makes it better.*

I love you. *I'm yours for as long as forever lasts.*

It helped, but it still didn't feel like enough. Not because she wasn't enough, or him, but maybe because after all he'd put her through, he needed something bigger than words. Some blunt-force miracle to crack open every last doubt.

Hell, even the secret of them being together felt more wrong than right.

What was it she'd told him last year? That so many times in

her life had felt like a battle. He wanted to change that, yet he couldn't fix the unfixable. He had Parkinson's. That was a battle she'd vowed to fight at his side.

But there had to be something else...

When the end of June rolled around, a wild idea took root in his brain. Big enough to make a point. Foolish enough it felt exactly right.

Because if he was going to stake his claim on destiny, he needed to do it where everyone could see.

Canada Day hit, and all his plans nearly went up in smoke when he barely made it to the old community hall on time. He arrived after lunch, and the bachelor auction had already begun when he slipped in the back door, heart hammering as he snuck onto the back of the stage.

The heat was oppressive, the thin light of a single overhead bulb barely breaching the darkness. The curtain was closed for some reason, and the scent of masculine sweat and nerves blended on the air.

From behind the curtain, Chance's voice rang out, pitched smooth and professional. "Come now. Do I have any other bids?"

Cody edged past a cluster of bachelors perched on folding chairs, all looking as if they'd rather be anywhere else. "What the hell is going on? Why are you sitting here in the dark?" he asked quietly.

One of them, a skinny cowboy he half-knew from the feed store, lifted a shoulder. "Curtain's stuck. Mr. Fields is grabbing us when it's our turn."

Before Cody could reply, a roar went up on the other side of the curtain. Voices overlapped. Laughter, a smattering of applause, a high, clear shout that sounded suspiciously like *I love you!*

Cody made a move toward the curtain to see what was

happening when Jose Sanchez, the stock manager from the seed and feed, slapped a hand onto his forearm and squeezed so tight Cody winced.

"Can't—breathe," Jose rasped, eyes wide and glassy.

"Shit." Cody dropped to his knees. "You have an inhaler? An EpiPen?"

Jose shook his head frantically. "No allergies—just...oh, damn—"

Not allergies. Panic attack then.

Cody had seen it a dozen times. Usually in kids forced too close to a horse or an arena full of screaming strangers. He didn't think twice. He braced a steady hand on Jose's shoulder.

"Hey. You're okay. Look at me."

Jose's gaze flicked up, eyes wild.

"Slow breaths," Cody coached, his voice low and even. "You're safe. Nothing here is going to hurt you."

The curtain shifted. Malachi's booming laugh rumbled over the chaos. "That's a twist I never saw coming. Never thought your first day on the job would be this exciting, did you, Chance?"

Chance sounded exasperated. "No, sir. Seems we have a bachelor in a hurry to collect his date. Let's get him out of here."

Cody held Jose's gaze another beat, waited for the man's breathing to steady. When his shoulders dropped fractionally, Cody gave him a nod and squeezed his arm.

"Stay here. You're okay."

Cody stood and determinedly headed for the front of the stage. He ducked around Malachi just as the older man eased into the back.

"Cody?" Malachi's brows rose.

"Later," Cody muttered. "I need to do something first."

He slipped through the curtain.

Chance turned, relief brightening his face until he saw who it was. "Oh, for fuck's sake."

"Good thing your mic is off," Cody deadpanned. He slapped Chance's shoulder, forcing a semblance of normalcy into his voice. "Crowd's starting to look confused. Get on with it."

Chance's jaw flexed. "What the hell are you doing, bro?"

"It's the only solution."

"The only—" Chance dragged a hand over his mouth. "You're about to hurt a wonderful woman."

"If I'm lucky," Cody said quietly, "I'm about to fix it."

Chance studied him a moment longer, then blew out a breath and turned to face the crowd.

"Now, as my future father-in-law explained, I'm still in training," he began, voice smooth again. "I hope you'll forgive one last mix-up. We have an unexpected last-minute bachelor. Well-known to you all. My brother."

Cody stepped forward and took the microphone. The stage lights hit him in the eyes, hot and blinding.

The noise swelled. A low buzz of curiosity and surprise. Someone near the front let out an excited whoop.

But none of that mattered.

He found Fern instantly in the crowd. She sat with Rose, an empty chair beside them. Her hands rested in her lap, her expression a quiet, controlled calm.

Those lips he'd kissed in the dark, soft and fierce and sure, were pressed together in a tight line. The eyes that had flashed with mischief and desire and faith—flat and unreadable.

God, he'd done that. He'd left her standing alone.

But he was about to fix all that.

He swallowed and forced the words out through the tight ache in his throat.

"Hey." His voice cracked. He cleared it. "I'm not officially on the auction list, but I'd like to offer myself up anyway."

His heart thumped, slow and certain.

One breath. Then another.

She deserved someone who could be brave. Who could say what he felt without waiting for her to guess it first.

The auction must have started. Cody had no idea, he was too busy staring into the future in Fern's eyes.

Chance cleared his throat. "Bidding stands at five hundred. Do I hear six?"

Voices rose. A woman Cody had dated years ago waved a hand, smiling too brightly.

Chance lifted his mic. "Bid stands at six-fifty, going once…"

Cody took a step closer to the crowd and found Fern's gaze again before he said, "Wait."

Everything hushed.

"I bid seven hundred."

Gasps. Then a chorus of incredulous laughter.

"You can't do that," Chance protested, though his mouth twitched. "Can you do that?"

Cody drew a shaky breath. "I just did. So obviously, it's possible." He turned fully toward Fern, intensely glad that everyone was watching. "I'm buying me for someone special. She's been trying to tell me what my heart already knew." He let out a shaky laugh. "I'm done fighting destiny."

For a second, no one moved.

Then Fern's smile broke like the dawn. Bright and unstoppable.

Everything in his chest unlocked.

He was hers. He'd always been.

Every fight, every time Fern had dug in her heels and refused to settle, had led her here. To Cody, on a stage he hadn't planned to stand on, bidding on himself in front of half the county.

For her.

Her heart didn't lurch this time. It lifted.

I'm done fighting destiny.

The crowd erupted. Applause and delighted laughter swelled, filling every dusty corner of the hall.

Fern didn't hear a bit of it.

She saw Cody. *Only* Cody, standing there in his plain button-up and jeans, hair a little too long from neglect, mouth curved in a shaky, incredulous smile.

It wasn't the smile of a man about to bolt. It was the look of someone who'd finally stopped running.

Her feet moved before her brain could catch up.

She stepped around Rose, who let out a choked little gasp, then carried on past the rest of the folding chairs. She reached the edge of the stage and braced her hand on the scuffed plywood riser.

She met Cody's gaze straight on. "I believe you're mine, cowboy."

Cody's eyes went wide. For a single beat, he just stared, as if he couldn't quite believe she was real.

A ripple of laughter rolled through the audience.

Behind the mic stand, Chance gave an exaggerated sigh. "Well, that seems settled, unless any of you ladies feel like bidding higher?"

A chorus of good-natured groans and a few halfhearted "no thanks!" rose up.

"Good." Fern swung herself onto the stage without hesitating, ignoring the hand Chance offered her. She didn't need help.

She needed *him.*

She crossed the worn floorboards in three strides. Cody still hadn't moved. His eyes were bright, almost dazed.

"You look as if you're waiting for lightning to strike," she murmured, low enough only he could hear.

"Feels like it already did," he rasped. "I didn't know how to make it right."

She reached for him, her strong hand pressed flat over the hard thump of his heart and smiled. "You just did."

She kissed him, slow and certain, and everything fell back into place.

The noise in the hall swelled. Cheers, applause, laughter, but she didn't care.

When she pulled back, she didn't drop her hand from his chest. She made sure he couldn't look away.

"You already made it right," she said again, clearer this time, so there was no chance he'd ever forget it.

Another hush swept through the crowd, just long enough to feel the weight of it, as if everyone there knew they were watching something inevitable.

Fern turned her head slightly, her voice carrying with perfect calm. "I'll be taking this one home. If that's all right."

Someone hollered, "Amen!" Another voice crowed, "About damn time!"

Cody let out a squeaky laugh. A sound so raw and relieved her heart squeezed.

Chance cleared his throat, his grin nearly splitting his face. "As much as I'd love to call it done, we do have other bachelors still hiding in the wings."

"Then we'll clear the stage," Fern said sweetly. She slid her hand into Cody's. Steady or not, she knew exactly how to hold him up.

Chance tipped an imaginary hat. "Be my guest."

And then, because she knew him down to the marrow, she turned back to Cody and lifted her chin. "Ready?"

His voice was rough but sure. "With you? Always."

Fern kept hold of him, refusing to give him even an inch of retreat. "Your truck?"

He nodded voice rough when he said, "Across the street."

She didn't let go until he'd unlocked the door. She climbed in with her heart battering her ribs.

Cody slid behind the wheel and just sat there. One hand still grasped her forearm. When he looked over, his eyes were glossy in the dim glow of the dash.

"I love you," he said hoarsely.

She let the words sink into her bones. Let them fill every crack his absence had left.

"Of course you do."

His laugh cracked on a sob.

"You scared me," she whispered.

"I scared myself."

Fern reached over and caught his cheek in her palm. "Drive me home."

He did.

Except he didn't take her to her house. He took her to his.

When she turned to look at him, questioning, Cody pressed his forehead to hers. "I'm so damn tired of pretending I can do this without you."

"You don't have to," she murmured.

He kissed her then. Slow, deep, everything he hadn't said with words.

They stumbled inside, neither of them bothering to turn on a light. She backed him against the closed door, threading her fingers into his hair, kissing him until she was dizzy.

"You sure?" he rasped.

"Surer than I've ever been about anything."

His mouth came down on hers again, hotter this time. Needy. His hands roamed her back, then her hips, tugging her flush against him.

Fern broke the kiss long enough to breathe, her voice soft and fierce. "I love you."

A tremor passed through him, not the kind she feared but something older, deeper. Relief so sharp it left him shuddering.

"I love you too," he repeated.

The words fell between them like a vow.

No more running. No more walls.

Cody kissed her like he'd never let her go again. His hands skated down her arms, sliding comfortably over the place where flesh changed to prosthesis. She pulled back just enough to look him in the eye.

"I know you're scared," she said. "Me too."

He nodded, breathing raggedly. "But you still want me?"

"I want *us*."

She pushed up on her toes and kissed him again. His mouth opened under hers, hungry and unguarded. His hands slid to her hips, then lower, hoisting her effortlessly. Her back hit the wall, and she wrapped her legs around him.

Every place they touched felt electric.

She cupped his face in both hands—her real one and her prosthetic one—and held him still, just long enough to whisper:

"You're mine. *Always*."

His answering groan vibrated through her, low and ragged.

"God, Fern," he breathed, voice thick with everything he didn't have words for.

She kissed him then, deep and sure, until neither of them could remember what it felt like to be uncertain.

When he carried her to his bedroom, she didn't look away. She didn't want to miss a second of this, of him.

When they finally sank into the bed together, she felt it

settle deep in her bones. This wasn't a temporary choice. It wasn't a fling doomed by fear or circumstance.

It was a commitment to tomorrow, however uncertain tomorrow might be.

They made love slowly, unhurried, each touch deliberate, like sealing a promise neither of them would ever take back.

When it was over, she curled into his side, her ear pressed over his heart. The steady thump anchored her, chased away every last scrap of doubt.

His hand rested on her bare arm, warm and careful. "Thank you," he whispered.

She smiled into his skin. "For what?"

"For being the best destiny a guy could ever hope for. For believing in me when I couldn't."

Fern closed her eyes, letting the quiet fill every aching corner inside her. "We'll believe together," she murmured.

Outside, the world kept spinning. Inside, they needed nothing but this.

Nothing but each other.

15

———————

Some days, Cody woke up and still felt the itch to run.

Old habits died hard, and the habit of bolting—of thinking the only way to protect people was to vanish—had a hold on him so deep he sometimes wondered if it was in his bones.

But he stayed.

He was learning that staying took a different kind of courage.

He sat down with Karen and Finn in early July, palms damp, heart thumping so hard he could barely hear himself.

"I don't know what my life is going to look like," he said quietly. "But as long as there's work I can do, I'm willing to be here for you."

He half-expected them to thank him for his honesty and start drawing up a plan to transition him out.

Instead, Karen smiled. Not kindly, but the way she smiled when she was about to hand someone their ass in a meeting. Finn just sat there, arms folded, eyes steady.

"Good," Karen said. "Because you're not going anywhere."

And just like that, he wasn't.

They upgraded him from his little cabin to a two-bedroom, told him any out-of-pocket medical expenses were covered by the ranch insurance, and reminded him that Red Boot had always been about family, not just payroll.

He'd gone home that day feeling lighter than he had in months.

Fern moved in the next week.

The Fields clan arrived in a convoy of trucks and SUVs, helping to haul in furniture, dishes, and Fern's collection of watercolour supplies.

Sophie and Malachi presented them with a wicker basket containing fresh bread wrapped in linen and a tin of coarse salt.

"It's a traditional blessing. May this house never know hunger, and may your life be full of flavour," Sophie said, eyes suspiciously bright.

Fern sniffled. "We're still going to come over to your house a lot," she warned.

"Of course you will," Malachi agreed. "But call first. You never know what your mother and I might be up to."

Cody didn't want to know why that made all the Fields girls snicker so hard. But he did appreciate how the cabin slowly and steadily became a home with Fern's caring touch.

Some mornings, she left early to go work at the gallery, carrying her laptop bag slung over her shoulder. She'd started painting more seriously, too, and now a watercolour of the wild horses hung framed above their bed.

Cody spent his days working the trail ride schedule, tending fences, and figuring out, one step at a time, how to plan for a future he couldn't fully see.

He took the medication he'd been prescribed. He listened to the tremor in his hand, tried not to hate it.

He tried to remember that even imperfect days were a gift.

On August 10th, he hosted Chance's bachelor party out at the ranch. The sky had been threatening rain since dawn, and by early evening, clouds roiled low and dark across the prairie. But no one cared.

They set up folding chairs around the fire pit. Music drifted over the fields, mingling with laughter, the scent of barbeque and beer on the air.

Chance looked as if he'd been waiting for this moment his whole life. Grinning, relaxed, surrounded by the people who'd become his own patchwork family.

Time for the working part of the evening, Cody decided. He rose to his feet, lifting his beer.

"To the demise of my brother's imminent solo status," he began, voice carrying on the breeze. "He's the best type of brother. The kind I would've picked myself, but I didn't have to because someone else in my family was smart enough to make that choice for me."

Chance's head dipped, a crooked smile softening his face.

Cody glanced around at the circle of faces, feeling the old ache in his chest ease. "So we have to thank our mom and dad first—for being smart enough to put us together."

Chance cleared his throat and raised his glass. "To your Ma and me Da," he agreed, accent thickening. "Best possible folks a man could choose." His grin sharpened. "And a toast to the Fields family—brave enough to welcome not one, but two Gabrielle men into their fold."

A ragged cheer went up, punctuated by a sharp crack of thunder overhead.

Lightning split the sky, bright as day for a heartbeat.

Then the wind came, rolling across the pasture in a wall of dust and cold.

"Inside!" someone yelled, and the chairs scraped over the grass as everyone bolted for the ranch house.

The storm hammered the roof in waves. Inside, though, the mood only got rowdier. Someone produced a deck of cards, and before long they were passing around whiskey and taking turns sharing stories about Chance. Most of them only half true, all of them hilarious.

Cody leaned back in his chair, feeling something he hadn't in a long time.

Peace.

He caught Chance watching him across the table, eyes bright with mischief.

"You're smiling," Chance observed. "That's suspicious."

"I was just thinking," Cody drawled, "that before you get legally tied down, you ought to shave off that ridiculous mustache."

Chance spluttered, then narrowed his eyes. "You serious?"

"Dead serious." Cody somehow kept a straight face. "Don't you know that it's tradition in Canada for you to be clean shaven for a wedding?"

His brother stared at him.

"Hey, ask anyone," Cody insisted. He glanced around. Brilliant. "Hey, Zach," he shouted across the noisy room. "Did you have whiskers on your wedding day, or were you clean shaved?"

"Which wedding?" some joker sang out. "The one where he was sober or the one when he was drunk?"

Zach flashed his middle finger at the guy before answering Cody's question. "Clean shaved. For both," he added with a grin.

"Thank you." Cody raised his beer in the air.

Chance went solemn, rubbing his jaw as if he was pondering the question of the century. "Hmmm. That's a decision not to be taken lightly."

"You have until the morning," Cody choked out, coughing lightly and rising to his feet. "Excuse me."

He had to get away before he broke into outright laughter. God, if his brother followed through, Rose was going to kill them both.

An hour later, Chance caught up with him as Cody stood on the covered deck and watched the storm rage over the mountains. "You're an eejit," Chance announced, mock affront and fond exasperation all tangled up in his expression. Then he swatted Cody's shoulder. "But I love you anyway."

"Feeling's mutual, brother."

"I'm not shaving." Chance's eyes softened. "Now show me the ring."

Cody blinked. "What ring?"

A colourful string of Irish curses filled the air.

"Oh," Cody said, fighting a grin. "*That* ring."

He reached into his pocket and pulled out the small velvet box.

Chance went quiet as Cody flipped it open. Inside, the simple band gleamed—a slim braid of white gold, nothing flashy.

"Fern is happy just being with me," Cody said, voice low. "But I want it official. I can't do much about what my body might do a year from now, or in ten years. But if I marry her, I can protect her the best I can and make sure her financial future's secure."

Chance looked up, expression unguarded. "She doesn't care about that, you know."

"I know." Cody closed the box. "But I do."

Chance nodded slowly. "You don't have to do any of it alone, Cody. You and Fern. You have all of us."

Cody swallowed, the knot in his throat too big to speak around.

Yeah.

For once, he knew it.

They stood there while the storm thundered, the house rang with laughter, and the sweet smell of wet prairie grass rose in the air.

In that moment, Cody realized he wasn't waiting to be whole anymore.

He already was.

~

IT POURED on Rose and Chance's wedding day.

Not a soft, romantic drizzle. A full-on, sideways-blowing, windows-rattling prairie storm.

Fern had watched the clouds drench the land all morning, hoping and pleading that the weather gods might have mercy long enough for the ceremony to take place in the backyard garden as planned.

But the heavens had other ideas.

When she finally gave up and climbed the stairs to the primary bedroom at their childhood home where Rose was getting ready, she found her sister standing at the window, rain pelting the glass in sheets, a blissed-out smile on her face.

"You're gorgeous," Fern told her honestly, stepping close to adjust the delicate ringlet resting on Rose's smooth black hair.

"I'm wet," Rose said, grinning wider as she gestured to her tear-stained cheeks. "I'm probably going to stay wet all day."

"You're radiant," Ivy corrected from her perch in the corner, a teacup balanced on the arm of her chair. She looked pale but content, the edges of her fragility smoothed by quiet satisfaction. "You're all so beautiful."

"Even me?" Tansy piped up, flopping dramatically back

into the upholstered chaise. Her casted leg stuck out at a ridiculous angle. "Because I'm only wearing one pretty shoe."

Fern snickered. "You're beautiful, even if your July first was a bit more exciting than mine."

Tansy nodded seriously and didn't deny it. "I'll take the broken leg, though, because it came with a happily-ever-after for more than just me."

Rose turned from the rain with a soft laugh, cradling her bouquet like a talisman. "Weather aside, it still feels perfect, you know?"

"It is perfect," Fern said, fiercely. "Every bit of it."

For a moment, they were all quiet, four women linked by love and a thousand shared memories.

Tansy reached out and wiggled her fingers. "Four Fields sisters. A whole bouquet of happiness."

Fern sat beside her, letting her palm rest over Tansy's.

"Speaking of bouquets," Rose murmured, extending hers into the circle. "Since I got to make it, I made exactly what I wanted. This is us."

They all leaned closer to look.

Ivy was there in the trailing vines of deep green, glossy and strong. Fern saw herself in the lacey fronds tucked among the roses—delicate but impossible to uproot. Tansy's bright yellow tansy flowers were a cheerful, unexpected burst against the softer pinks of the roses.

"I remember," Tansy said, voice low, "when I first came to live with Mom and Dad. They told me if I wanted, I could choose a new name. Something that fit better than the one I'd had. I wanted a flower name, like all of you."

Fern swallowed around the lump in her throat. She'd been too young for her own memories of the time, but she knew the stories and could picture it. Tansy at twelve. So wary, yet so hungry to belong.

"But I didn't want something perfect," Tansy continued. "So I picked a weed."

"You didn't pick a weed," Fern corrected gently. "You picked a flower that grows wherever it damn well pleases. One that brightens up everything around it."

Tansy's eyes shimmered. "That's nice. I'll pretend you didn't just call me stubborn."

"I did," Fern admitted, smiling. "But it's true."

Ivy lifted her cup in a toast. "To all of us. Stronger together."

Rose reached over to squeeze her hand. "Thank you all for standing with me today."

Fern's heart felt too full to speak. She just nodded.

A knock at the door startled them. Walker poked his head in. "Showtime."

They assembled in the front foyer instead of the garden—no one was brave enough to risk the storm.

Yet the tempest became a part of the ceremony in a unique and beautiful way. Malachi stood to one side of the open double front doors, the rain pouring down outside in a silver curtain. The foyer filled up fast, and the rooms to either side were filled with people who sat or stood to watch. Guests lined one side of the stairs and leaned on the second-story balcony, peering over the railing.

Chance waited by the entrance, mustache and beard neatly trimmed, his hair combed into place, his grin unstoppable.

Cody stood just behind him, wearing his best jacket. His expression caught somewhere between wonder and something else Fern couldn't quite name.

Then she figured that he was staring at her.

Fern lifted her chin.

Her shoes were slightly damp in the toes. Her hair was

curlier than usual in the high humidity. She didn't care. It wasn't about how any of them looked right then. Not really.

The love filling the four walls of her home to overflowing was the star of the event.

She crossed the foyer and took her place opposite Cody, her heart hammering.

Malachi cleared his throat, voice warm and steady as he began the vows. "To love, and to care. To hold each other through uncertainty, through every minute of every day. That's the promise being made today."

Her father continued, then Chance and Rose spoke. Fern heard them, she did, but she couldn't drag her gaze off Cody.

His hand twitched at his side. Not the familiar tremor but something different.

Slowly, deliberately, he lifted it.

A small velvet box sat in his palm.

He raised one brow, eyes locked on hers in a question so obvious it made her lungs seize.

Seriously? she mouthed, her heart flipping.

His mouth twitched, the corner of it lifting.

She pressed her lips together to hold in the laugh. This man. This impossible, stubborn, *wonderful* man.

"You may kiss the bride!" Malachi announced.

The crowd erupted. Rose and Chance turned to each other, the whole world narrowing into that first sweet moment as husband and wife.

And Cody...

Cody didn't hesitate.

He darted around the kissing newlyweds, straight into Fern's space, and swept her off her feet.

She let out a startled laugh, wrapping her arms around his neck as he spun her in a tight circle, the foyer blurring around them.

Joy poured down the stairs, danced through the archways, and mingled with the claps and cheers.

When Cody set her back on her feet, his hands lingered on her waist.

His voice was quiet, rough with feeling. "I love you."

Fern closed her fingers around the front of his shirt. "Damn right you do."

His smile flashed bright. "I don't have a speech ready. Or a plan. But I have this."

He opened the little box.

Inside, a slim ring gleamed. A simple band of white gold, nothing fancy.

She stared at it, her heart thudding so hard it hurt.

"You really want to do this here?" she whispered.

"Where better?" His voice cracked. "I'm done trying to pretend I don't know what I want."

Fern let out a breathless, wobbly laugh. "Are you going to ask me properly?"

His thumb traced her cheek. "Marry me?"

She didn't need to think. She pressed her forehead to his, eyes closing as the last of her fear and sadness fell away.

"Yes."

The cheering around them swelled until it felt as if the walls might burst.

He kissed her, soft and sure, and when they finally pulled back, she grinned at him through tears.

"Someday," she said, voice low and shaking with joy, "we're going to have a long talk about your sense of timing."

"Deal," Cody whispered. His hand tightened around hers. "But before we have that talk, you want to get married right now? Since everyone's already here?"

A giant burst of laughter escaped her. She took a moment to catch her breath before turning to her father.

"Daddy," she said, her voice strong. "Do you have a minute?"

Malachi examined her carefully as Rose and Chance crowded closer, eyes wide.

"Fern and I would like to get married," Cody said, meeting each of their eyes squarely. "If Chance and Rose don't mind us stealing a little of their thunder."

"About time, you eejit," Chance said, but his grin flashed as bright as the lightning outside the open door. Rose threw her arms around Fern, hugging her tight.

Malachi blinked then broke into a broad, astonished smile.

"Everyone stay put," he called to the curious onlookers. "Seems we have one more celebration to complete."

Outside, the rain kept falling. Inside, everything finally felt right.

Fern had met her destiny, and he was perfect.

New York Times Bestselling Author Vivian Arend
invites you to Heart Falls. After the story is done, their stories
go on. This series of vignettes and novellas are set in the world
of Heart Falls and feature previous couples and other side
characters.

Heart Falls Vignette and Novella Collection
Three Weddings And A Baby
Girls' Night Out
Rose's One Night to Forever
Fern's Date with Destiny
Hot Nights in Heart Falls

The Stones of Heart Falls
A Rancher's Heart
A Rancher's Song
A Rancher's Bride
A Rancher's Love
A Rancher's Vow

The Colemans of Heart Falls
The Cowgirl's Forever Love
The Cowgirl's Secret Love
The Cowgirl's Chosen Love

ABOUT THE AUTHOR

New York Times and *USA Today* bestselling author Vivian Arend loves to share the products of her over-active imagination with her readers. She writes contemporary, western, and light-hearted paranormal romances. The stories are humorous yet emotional, usually with a large cast of family or friends, and a guaranteed happily-ever-after. Vivian lives in British Columbia, Canada, with her husband of many years—her inspiration for every hero and a willing companion for all sorts of adventures.

www.vivianarend.com